'Get in the bath or I'll put you in it myself,' Tomas said softly.

That order melted the last frozen part within Zara.

'Really?' She couldn't help smiling at him. 'How d'you think you're going to do that?'

He looked up at her for just a moment longer, his focus dipping to her mouth. Then suddenly, in one smooth movement, he caught both her wrists in one of his hands and to her astonishment swiftly lifted his jumper and pressed her cold, cold fingers to his bare skin.

She gasped at the shock—and the sensation. She looked up into his face and saw how intently he was gazing at her.

'Tomas…' she whispered. Pleading. She couldn't help it.

He didn't reply. He just stepped that last inch closer and kissed her.

She moaned in instant delight, despite the fact his kiss was furious. He subjected her to the full force of his anger—and his passion—and both only brought forth the desire she'd tried to hold within herself for so long.

She moaned again, her legs weakening, but he abruptly broke the kiss.

Never had a man made her feel like this. Made her *want* like this.

He stared down at her silently, his breathing quick, his expression burning. But he didn't smile back at her.

'Go and get into the bath,' he breathed, releasing her completely. 'Go. *Now.*'

'Y-yes,' she stammered. Then turned and fled.

Natalie Anderson adores a happy ending. So you can be sure you've got a happy ending in your hands right now—because she promises nothing less. Along with happy endings she loves peppermint-filled dark chocolate, pineapple juice and extremely long showers. Not to mention spending hours teasing her imaginary friends with dating dilemmas. She tends to torment them before eventually relenting and offering—you guessed it—a happy ending. She lives in Christchurch, New Zealand, with her gorgeous husband and four fabulous children. If, like her, you love a happy ending, be sure to come and say hi on Facebook—facebook.com/authornataliea—follow @authornataliea on Twitter, or visit her website/blog: natalie-anderson.com.

Books by Natalie Anderson

Mills & Boon Modern Romance

Tycoon's Terms of Engagement
Blame It on the Bikini

The Throne of San Felipe

The Mistress that Tamed De Santis
The Secret That Shocked De Santis

Mills & Boon Modern Tempted

Whose Bed Is It Anyway?
The Right Mr Wrong
Waking Up in the Wrong Bed
First Time Lucky?

Visit the Author Profile page
at millsandboon.co.uk for more titles.

THE FORGOTTEN
GALLO BRIDE

BY
NATALIE ANDERSON

MILLS
BOON

HarperCollins
P U B L I S H E R S
Since 1817

First Published in Great Britain 2017
By Mills & Boon, an imprint of HarperCollins*Publishers*
1 London Bridge Street, London, SE1 9GF

© 2017 Natalie Anderson

ISBN: 978-0-263-06850-4

Printed and bound in Great Britain
by CPI Antony Rowe, Chippenham, Wiltshire

THE FORGOTTEN
GALLO BRIDE

For Toni—thank you.

CHAPTER ONE

'Type the security code quickly and get through the gates before he sees you, or he'll override the system and won't let you in. Don't get there after dark or you haven't a hope...'

ZARA FALCONER SQUINTED through the relentless rain, mentally reciting the long code while struggling to hold her freezing fingers steady enough to tap it into the keypad. Because of the storm clouds the sky had darkened early and Jasper's warning rang loudly in her ears.

Nervously she entered the last number he'd given her and held her breath, but the heavy wrought-iron gates remained as tight-locked as ever. She glanced back at the keypad, wondering if she should try again. A sudden loud clang told her she didn't need to.

The gates creaked more as they slowly opened, complaining they were unused to the movement. Zara didn't trust them to remain open for long. The *DO NOT ENTER* and *TRESPASSERS WILL BE PROSECUTED* signs pretty much gave it away. She hurried back to her car, slithering on the wet path in her haste. She inhaled deeply and tried to move more calmly. She'd only just driven through the gap when the iron gates began to close again behind her, groaning as they locked back into their defensive position.

She switched her windscreen wipers onto a faster setting and put her headlights on full to try to see more clearly where she was going. Her breathing quickened as the wet gravel crunched beneath her tyres. Big, barren branches from the large trees overhead obscured the bruised, weeping sky. She inched her battered old car down the long driveway, taking the corner at the end. That was when she had her first glimpse of the large Georgian manor that was his home. With its two stories of imposing bricks and empty windows, it was a vast, gloomy obstruction at the end of the drive. The whole building was in darkness save a feeble light gleaming in only one low window.

Her heart pounded as she pulled up right in front of the mammoth front door. She'd been driving all day and couldn't quite believe she was finally here. She'd tried to imagine this moment every day for the past year, envisaging all kinds of possible scenarios—maybe she'd bump into him on the street, or maybe they'd be at an event together and see each other across a room, or maybe he'd come to find *her*...

She'd really had no idea how it was going to happen or indeed if it ever actually would. But then Jasper had found her and basically got on his knees and begged her to visit the man to whom they both owed so much. Jasper's tired appearance and desperation had surprised her. He didn't know she needed no real encouragement to see the man who'd changed her life so drastically. She wanted to. Secretly she'd been aching to for months.

So now here she was with her shoes and jeans wet, her hair a straggly mess, and she was late...but she was *here*.

She grabbed her bag and got out of the car but, despite running to the door, only got more drenched. She no longer cared. She was too busy wondering how he'd react to seeing her again. Would he smile and laugh? Would he look concerned and caring? What would he say?

Unable to suppress the scared-but-excited shivers running up and down her spine, Zara rang the doorbell. She bit her lower lip but she couldn't stop the shy smile from slipping across her face. They'd had such a short encounter, but it had changed everything in her life. She'd relived those precious moments every day since. And every day she'd longed for just a few more.

She didn't hear any footsteps over the thumping of her own pulse. It seemed that the door just silently swung open without any warning. And then he was standing in the doorway frowning down at her.

Tomas Gallo.

All she could do was stare.

He was taller than she remembered, and leaner-looking in his faded black jeans and thin black sweater. His hair wasn't now cut in that perfect, almost preppy, business-man's style, instead it was longer, a jet-black unruly mess with a hint of curl that ended just above his collar. Despite his olive skin, he was pale. There was no Caribbean holiday tan on him now. Not that devilish smile either. He hadn't shaved in a couple of days and the stubble emphasised the sharp edges and planes of his jaw. He looked harder, unhappier. But his eyes were the same—still that beautiful dark brown. The soulful kind of eyes that you could look into for ever, but still never understand the secrets they held. And there were definitely secrets. Even more of them.

He was so striking and so unforgettable. In that one second he stole her breath—and her heart—all over again.

'What?' he snapped as she stood there speechlessly staring at him.

Her shy offer of a smile froze.

'How did you get in here?' He glared down at her, clearly expecting an immediate answer.

She wasn't able to give him one. She wasn't able to speak at all. She watched him closely for a hint of recognition in his eyes, but there was only mistrust—and building anger.

'I don't know how you got inside the gates,' he added roughly, 'but the gardens haven't been open to the public in almost a year.'

'I'm not here to see the gardens,' she finally managed to answer.

'Then what are you doing here?' He continued to glare at her. There was no recognition, no softness, no humanity.

The smile faded from her lips altogether. Awkwardly she stared back up at him. Jasper had said it was better to arrive unannounced. That he wouldn't tell Tomas she was coming. But did he *really* not remember her?

She knew she'd changed, but it was only clothes, a new hairstyle...she didn't think such superficial things would have made that much difference.

'I don't want whatever it is you're selling.' He began to shut the door.

That galvanised her into action. She'd not driven all day in such horrendous conditions to be given the brush-off in the first two seconds. In that way, she *had* changed.

'I'm not here to sell you anything,' she said, boldly stepping forward and blocking the doorway. 'I'm here to help you.'

For a beat he looked stunned before snapping back, 'I don't need help.'

Defiantly she stood exactly where she was, uncaring that she was getting wet; she was not walking away from this just yet.

'Yes, you do,' she argued, taking another step forward right into the doorway. 'Jasper sent me to you.'

Jasper had told her Tomas was still recovering from the accident. That he needed more help than he liked to admit. And while Tomas might not want her assistance, she owed him for more than he'd ever know and she wanted to pay him back for that.

He looked her over again, more slowly that time. There was still not the recognition in his expression that she'd expected, but as she watched something else emerged— something raw.

'I don't need or want your help,' he said slowly, cynicism harsh in his eyes.

She tried not to be insulted, but she failed. 'You don't even know what I can do for you.'

'I'm not interested in anything that you think you can do for me, sweetheart.' A bitter smile curved his lips as he glanced over her again. He looked so thoroughly and slowly it was as if the rains had stripped her naked and he could see every tiny intimate detail of her body.

Embarrassed heat stormed through her as his gaze lingered on her breasts. She fought hard to control her reaction to his perusal but sensual awareness circled around her, fogging everything.

'Excuse me?' she choked, stunned at her own horrendous reaction.

'What is it you're offering?' he asked. 'A massage?'

'You think I'm here to give you a massage?' she asked, utterly astonished.

'And other…services as required.' Now he was looking at her mouth with a dark gleam in his eye.

She could feel herself blushing, she could almost see into his mind and knew exactly where he thought she might use her mouth on him…and the dreadful thing was, the truly dreadful thing was, she'd once dreamt about that. But she'd rather die before she admitted that—even to herself.

'Does Jasper usually send women to provide these "services" for you?' she asked huskily.

'No.' He frowned suddenly, that gleam vanishing, as if he too rejected the idea outright. 'This is…unexpected, even for him.'

She drew herself up, gaining less than an inch in height and she was still far from being able to look him straight in the eye, but it was better than shrinking in front of him. She wasn't that naive girl any more. She wasn't afraid to stand up for herself now. She wasn't going to run away and hide. 'I'm not here to provide you with intimate entertainment.'

His gaze clashed with her own fierce one. Something changed within his expression. Then he too straightened.

'What did Jasper say to you?' he asked harshly, even angrier now.

'That you were going to be alone this weekend.'

'And he thinks that's a problem?' he asked bitterly. 'Does he think I can't handle being alone?'

'You'd have to ask him that,' she answered crossly. 'I'm just doing what he asked me to.'

'Well, Jasper was mistaken in asking you to do anything for me. I apologise for my crass assumption. You may leave.'

It couldn't have sounded less like an apology. The sky was darkening more and she could see less of his face but she could sense his anger and his resistance to her presence. Her own anger bubbled. That he could be so rude? Had he truly forgotten her? She didn't care if he couldn't cope on his own or not, he didn't look remotely incapacitated to her. As far as she was concerned, Jasper was worrying about nothing and she couldn't wait to get out of the place. But she couldn't get past him not recognising her. 'Don't you know who—?'

But it was then that the heavens truly opened, turning from torrential rain to ice. Marble-sized hailstones pelted down, bouncing on the gravel and her car and creating such a din she could no longer hear herself think let alone catch a word of what he was now saying. She saw him mutter something else—most likely impolite—then he stepped back and held his arm out towards her.

Was he inviting her in now?

Furious, she didn't move. He sent her such a speaking look and then reached for her. His grip on her upper arm was hard and her feet were moving before she'd thought better of it. The door slammed behind her, shutting out the worst of the icy racket. But it was colder indoors than it had been out there. Her heart pounded. He'd stepped back only enough to drag her inside and suddenly they were face to face and only a couple of inches apart, his grip on her wasn't any less ferocious and she could feel his breath on her frozen face.

Her gaze clashed with his. In the dim light she could see little of his expression, only that it was harsh. Her breathing—and her pulse—quickened at his nearness. Her body remembered his touch and she shivered.

Abruptly he released her. As he turned away his hand brushed hers and she quivered again as that electricity arced into her.

Yes. For her, he'd always packed a punch.

'You may wait in here, until the hail has stopped,' he said stiffly, taking another step back from her, frowning down at his hand before turning to switch on the light.

She blinked as the sudden brightness hurt her eyes—as did his silence. Shaken by her intense reaction to his proximity, she decided it was better to stay silent herself.

He didn't invite her into a warm room and offer her a seat or a drink or anything more comfortable, only shelter from the storm that should hopefully pass quickly overhead.

It was clear he didn't want to wait with her, yet he didn't want to leave her alone in his large, inhospitable house either. She suppressed a vicious smile at his quandary, still smarting from his lack of recognition of her.

A year ago she'd seen him smile and heard him laugh as he'd joked with Jasper. From her hidden corner she'd been so drawn to him. He'd been arrogant then too, confident and assured, but it was different now—cold disapproval radiated from every inch of his body. He didn't want the intrusion. He didn't want her.

Well, he'd *never* wanted her. And that was just fine, wasn't it?

Except there'd been one moment all those months ago. One moment when he'd teased her, smiled at her, reassured her. And then come close to her. Her cheeks burned at the memory of just how close he'd gotten to her then. He'd taken her by surprise—and her own reaction?

'Miss—?'

He interrupted her thoughts, dragging her back to the cold, miserable presence.

He was staring, his eyebrows raised slightly as if he was wondering what she was thinking. Embarrassed, she glanced around the vast interior. It was freezing and so unwelcoming.

'Falconer.' She told him her new name. 'Zara Falconer.'

She looked back at him as she spoke but there was no reaction at all in his expression.

And there was no outward sign of injury either. He seemed perfectly capable of taking care of himself. Yet Jasper had been adamant that Tomas needed her. He'd been agitated about it. And curiosity had been too much for her.

Tomas was undeniably the same lethally attractive man, but the shadows in his face were deeper and darker. He didn't look like the carefree, rapier-sharp devil she'd met that day.

'Jasper asked me to housekeep for you for a few days,' she finally, formally explained her mission.

'You're too young.' He dismissed the idea in an instant.

She bristled, a bitter smile twisting her lips. How many times had she heard that in her life? Yes, she did look younger than she was, but she wasn't stupid and she could work as hard as anyone. In fact, she could work harder. She had for years. 'I'm not as young as I look.'

* * *

Tomas stared down at the bedraggled woman standing in front of him. She might think otherwise but he knew what Jasper's intentions had been in sending her to him. The old schemer had been insisting for months that what Tomas really needed was some fun times with a beautiful woman. That if he relaxed, it would all come right, but his old friend was completely wrong. And the minute he got rid of her, he'd be phoning Jasper to tell him so. Again.

But it surprised him that Jasper had sent someone so unlike the usual high-maintenance-model bombshell that the old man himself preferred. This girl was too sweet. She looked so damned young in those thin sneakers, wet jeans and the light jacket that didn't offer sufficient protection from the rain and annoyed the hell out of him. But as he looked closer he saw she was right. She wasn't quite as young as her appearance first suggested.

When Tomas had opened that door she'd had a shy smile on her glowing face. The rain had been like dew on her radiant skin. Her loosely tied back rich brown hair had been starting to tumble, so wet tendrils curled softly at her temples. Her sweetheart-shaped face was dominated by those large sea-green shining eyes and full rosebud lips. Hell, she'd even had a dimple when she smiled. She'd looked the very picture of innocence and *joie de vivre*.

Everything he wasn't. Everything he'd never had.

Right now she looked the picture of indignation. It was no less attractive and he was finding it very hard to wrench his eyes off her.

His thoughts were appallingly sexual in nature. He'd taken one look at her and been hit by the almost irresistible urge to draw her close and kiss her—and made a fool of himself in thinking that was why she'd come here. But her mouth looked full and soft and perfect for kissing and she was just the right size to fit in his arms and press against his hard body. He ached for that even now.

He couldn't remember when he'd last kissed a woman. Or last wanted to. But then, he couldn't remember anything.

Angered, he stepped towards her, not stopping even as her eyes widened in wary surprise. He didn't want to know why she was here making a small puddle on the hall floor as the water streamed from her stupidly light jacket. He didn't want to be bothered by how frozen her fingers had felt when the back of his hand had brushed against them. He didn't want to see those still-shining eyes casting their innocent, cautious appeal at him.

He didn't want to want her.

What he wanted was for her to be gone.

'How do you know Jasper?' His voice still sounded rusty. No real surprise given he hadn't spoken to anyone in two days, not even a quick phone call.

She looked uncomfortable and didn't answer. His eyes narrowed. What didn't she want to tell him? Was she *Jasper's* latest little affair? His anger flared irrationally. He forced himself to breathe evenly and assess the facts. She wasn't Jasper's type. And given the way she'd blushed before at his out of order assumption, she wasn't the type at all.

'He helped me out with something a while back,' she eventually answered evasively. 'Have you eaten dinner?'

'That's not your concern.' But even as he answered his stomach growled. He wondered if *she'd* eaten. She looked as if she could do with something hot and filling. Where the hell had she driven from anyway? And why? And he did not want to be wondering about her like this.

She walked the length of the hall, not bothering to hide her curiosity behind a veil of politeness. 'The house is dark and cold.'

Her tone wasn't judgmental but he felt argumentative. 'Maybe I like it that way.'

'You like to make it as unwelcoming as possible?' She flashed that impish smile as she turned back to face him. 'Are you that afraid of people?'

The edgy question was softened not so much by that smile as the shining candour in her eyes but it didn't defuse his simmering anger.

'I work hard and I don't like interruptions,' he corrected, refusing to be melted by her radiance, refusing to be drawn nearer to her. But the pull was powerful. He glared, infuriated by his primary, base response to her. 'And I don't need a baby-faced babysitter. It really is time for you to leave.'

Except he couldn't help wondering where she would go.

Her smile faded and a confused look entered her eyes, dulling the sea-green brilliance. Stupidly he felt he'd disappointed her in some way. He didn't like it.

'I'm not as young as you seem to think,' she suddenly declared with a lift to her chin, as if she'd made up her mind about something and was determined to see it through. 'I was married once.'

He huffed out a breath, stunned that her words wounded him in a niggling way. 'But you're not now?' he replied softly. The silence hung with significance.

Her eyelids dropped and she looked down, as if it hurt to hold his gaze. 'I guess it wasn't meant to be.'

'I'm sorry,' Tomas said stiffly. Not so innocent then; she'd been bruised. The thought of her being hurt grated on his already strained nerves.

He cursed Jasper for sending her to him.

He walked back to the front door, but when he opened it he saw that, while the hail had stopped, the rain had returned. It was almost completely dark now and it would be impossible for her to see three feet in front of her while driving. No way could he let her leave in this weather. Inwardly he cursed more.

'It isn't safe for you to leave tonight,' he said gruffly. 'You'll have to stay here.'

He looked at her again and something stirred in the back of his mind. Had he said those words to her before?

He scowled at the *déjà vu*—the trick of a feeble mind.

He loathed it when it happened. Hated thinking there might be a memory just out of reach and that there was nothing he could do to draw it closer or clearer. The most random, inconsequential things sparked it. He paused, waiting, hoping the fragment would float to the forefront of his mind.

It didn't. It never did.

Frustration flamed his anger to fury. He stepped towards her, his gaze narrowing. The shine in her eyes had gone. So had her smile.

'Do I know you?' He rapped the question, like machine-gun fire, hating that he was compelled to ask. Hated giving his weakness away.

'No,' Zara answered baldly, her throat aching from holding back her disappointment. She'd tried to prompt him just then, but it seemed that what had happened a year ago had been so minor that he'd forgotten it. He'd forgotten her.

She knew it was stupid to feel it, but the reality of her insignificance crushed her. Yet what had she expected? This wasn't a fairy tale. It never had been and never would be. It had been one afternoon, one night, one morning. It had been nothing to him, not even worth remembering.

And she hadn't just lied. He *didn't* know her. He never truly had.

But that hadn't stopped him from marrying her.

CHAPTER TWO

'I want your niece.'

IT HAD BEEN for less than two days and it had been total madness. But it had been real. They'd married.

She should try again to remind him outright, but she was too mortified. That year's worth of imaginings, of meeting him again and hoping to change his first impression of her? That she could show she was no longer that weak woman who'd needed rescuing—that she was strong and capable and going places—that kernel of hope that he might see her in a different light?

She'd been so stupid.

She had to get away from him—from here—immediately.

She stepped towards the still-open doorway, but before she got there he closed it and faced her, blocking the exit.

'You'll stay here for the night and travel on in the morning when the weather has eased,' he said.

His dictatorial tone checked her momentarily, but she held her ground. 'And if it hasn't eased?'

'You'll at least be able to see in the light.'

'My car has good headlights, I think it's better if I leave now.' The last thing she wanted was to stay here.

'No.' His tone brooked no argument.

She remembered that implacable decisiveness and the air of authority so very well. Once he'd made his mind up that was it. Done. He couldn't be crossed or fought. She'd seen that when he'd dispatched the argument of her uncle with an icy blade. And there was that weak part of her that still wanted his recognition to come.

'If you'd care to show me the kitchen,' she said coldly. 'The least I can do is make some supper for us both.'

And she'd be on the phone to Jasper as soon as she was alone.

'I don't need anything, but please help yourself to anything you may like,' he replied equally coolly.

He refrained from indulging in a smile of satisfaction, but that obvious restraint made her all the more annoyed. He was too used to getting his own way.

'You must be hungry after your journey,' he added formally.

He was determined to reject her assistance in any way, yet was insistent she accept his help. It was an arrogantly unfair power play. He'd ensured she was reliant on him, yet he refused any assistance or even kindness from her.

One day she'd make him accept it somehow, some time. Just for once she didn't want to be the weak one.

She followed him down the long cold corridor. In the light she now noticed a very slight limp as he walked.

'My office is on the second floor, but the kitchen is this way,' he explained briefly. 'Where have you driven from today, Zara?'

'Up north,' she answered carefully.

She was hyper aware of the latent strength in his lean physique as she followed him. He seemed more ruthless, he smiled a whole lot less, but he was still breathtaking. She'd forgotten just how much he fascinated her. Fortunately he didn't appear to realise the effect he had on her. Thank goodness. He'd never noticed how he made her feel.

Her heart thudded at the strangeness of this arrangement. She shouldn't have agreed to come. He didn't need her help at all—what had Jasper been worrying about?

'I'm sorry if I've inconvenienced you,' she said politely,

still trying to get over the smarting hurt that he'd not remembered her.

'I will ensure there is a room ready for you,' he replied and left her.

She watched as he left. Not big on small talk, was he?

The kitchen was beautiful and scrupulously clean and she realised she needed food. She'd think better if she warmed up. She'd prepare something and then speak to Jasper.

She checked the cupboards. There were barely the staples in the pantry. She opened the freezer and found a stack of containers—single-serve portions—labelled with the dish and the date it had been made, but also the date for him to eat. Someone had prepared enough for him to last the next few days. Who had done that, when Jasper had insisted that Tomas's housekeeper had walked out suddenly, leaving him in the lurch?

Someone had organised this for him. She frowned. So why had Jasper been so insistent she come then, if he'd already been taken care of?

Her frown deepened as she looked in the fridge. There was milk and another—uneaten—prepared whole meal, but no raw ingredients.

But the meal he was supposed to have eaten last night was still in there. So was the container labelled as his lunch. She glanced at the counter and the sink again; there wasn't even a drop of water from the tap in the bottom of the sink. If he'd prepared anything for himself, he'd not left a single sign of it.

She shrugged, telling herself not to care. But she would make herself—and him—something to warm up.

She took off her jacket and scrabbled round in the bottom of her shoulder bag and found the bar of plain chocolate she had there. Thank goodness she'd not eaten it on the drive down. She found a copper pan and gently warmed the milk on the stovetop and grated the chocolate in. As she stirred it to melt the slivers she couldn't stop the memories from tormenting her. She'd made him coffee that morning, served it with her special lemon-slice cake—that first recipe she'd ever tweaked.

'He's here to invest in the casino—don't screw it up. Stay out of sight as much as possible.'

By then she'd got good at staying out of sight. Her uncle's temper had been worsening by the day and she was the easiest person for him to vent it on. So she knew when to avoid him, but that day he'd needed her skills.

She'd been the only child of doting parents who'd died when she was just twelve. Her only living relative had flown in to console her. Uncle Charles had said he lived on a luxury yacht in Antigua and ran a casino. He'd sold her parents' home and told her she'd love it on his boat, with his glamorous second wife.

But that wife had walked out ten months later, fed up with the chauvinistic abuse he served up twenty-four-seven. She'd left teenaged Zara there alone to witness the drinking and womanising and gambling and sleaze.

Her uncle had blamed her for his wife's departure. In the end everything was her fault. That flashy 'home' had offered no relief from isolation and grief—it only exacerbated it, because she didn't fit the mould.

She'd been nothing but a disappointment to her uncle and he'd let her know it. She'd been so scared and lonely she'd let him stomp all over her—had shut herself away like some sad Cinderella. She'd been so stupidly quiet and shy.

She'd never been able to live up to the expectations he had of her. He'd told her time and time again she was useless. He refused to send her to school and begrudged the correspondence-school paperwork she requested.

She'd retreated below deck. Len, the Scottish chef he employed, became her one true friend and mentor. Over the next few years he'd taught her everything he knew. But then Charles sacked Len and told Zara to take over the food prep full time. At the time she'd thought it had been to spite her, but in hindsight she realised it was one of several signs of the financial failure he was verging on.

By then she'd long since lost contact with her school friends. She was isolated, lonely and trapped; her uncle held her passport and was the sole trustee of her finances—and the money her parents had left her?

All gone. Didn't she know how much it had cost her uncle to house her? Wasn't she grateful for that?

Her uncle Charles had been embarrassed that *she'd* had to wait on his unexpected, important guests. She wasn't decorative enough—not thin enough, not perfect enough. Not for investment guru, Tomas Gallo, and his lawyer, Jasper Danforth. She was the useless, mousy niece he'd inherited and had never wanted.

But for that business meeting she'd had to be the hostess as well as prepare the coffee and cakes. When she'd caught sight of Tomas Gallo as she'd carried the tea tray into the room, she'd nearly dropped everything.

He'd not appeared to notice when she spilt some of the coffee, but he'd eaten some of the lemon slice. Two pieces in fact.

She'd sat in the corner, mute, suffering silently as her uncle had made joke after joke at her expense. She'd been bowled over by Tomas's appearance and the bottomless depths of his eyes. He was the most striking man she'd ever seen but he and Jasper had appeared amused, as if they'd agreed with every one of her uncle's words. And she'd died that bit inside to see that someone so gorgeous could be so cruel.

Almost an hour had passed when Tomas had dropped the bombshell.

'Sorry, Charles, I don't think the casino is the right fit for us at this time.'

Her uncle had been beyond furious at losing the investment. He'd been unable to contain his rage, venting it on her down in the galley while the two guests upstairs were readying to leave. She'd stared at the floor as he'd berated her in a bitter hoarse whisper.

'You're worse than useless. If you were attractive you could have seduced him. But as if any man would ever want you. You're a millstone, you ungrateful, lazy little cow. You can't even pour a coffee properly.'

The blow had come sudden and hard. It had stung so much.

She'd run from the galley only to collide in the corridor with Tomas Gallo. She'd gasped, appalled that he was down there—that he might have heard…

Firm hands held her upper arms and she flinched when she looked into his thunderous face. He quickly stepped back into the side room, lifting her with him and swiftly closing the door behind them.

'Don't be afraid,' he muttered harshly.

But the lethal anger in his eyes told her he was so very much more dangerous than her uncle. He visibly made himself relax and force a small smile. That was when she realised his fury was not for her.

'He hit you.' He tilted her chin and inspected the red of her upper cheek.

'It doesn't matter.' She wanted him to leave before her uncle found out he was down here and made everything worse.

'It always matters,' he replied curtly.

Her heart was his in that second.

Tomas released her and she dashed the tears away with

*the back of her hand, willing him to go back up to the deck
and leave with his lawyer. But he didn't.*

*'You've lived here how long?' he abruptly asked. 'How
long?' he prompted when she didn't answer.*

'Almost ten years,' she whispered.

'You have money?'

She shook her head.

'Passport?'

'My uncle...' She trailed off hopelessly.

'I see.'

Yes, she'd known he saw more than she'd ever wanted anyone to see—not only had he seen through her uncle's 'joking' façade to the emotional abuse that it was symptomatic
of, he'd witnessed the occasional physical violence her uncle
subjected her to. She'd hated that she hadn't the strength
or resources to leave, she'd loathed the depth of her depen-
dence on her uncle. Flushing with mortification, she'd made
to push past Tomas but he'd grabbed her arm again. She'd
been forced to meet his gaze. There she'd read the steel and
the concern, the sympathy and—to her shock—empathy.

It was as if he'd understood, because he'd been there
himself.

But that had to have been her own projection. She'd
wanted out for so long, but she'd become so trapped by
imposed gratitude, felt so beholden and been so downtrod-
den, she hadn't known which way to turn or how to get
herself out of it. She'd had no money, no chance to study,
or to work. She'd been made to feel as if she owed Uncle
Charles everything.

'Do you want out?' Tomas asked bluntly.

*'Out?' She blinked uncomprehendingly. 'You mean do
I want to leave?'*

'Yes. Do you want me to help you?'

His question was brusque and unexpected. She instinctively knew he wasn't going to wait for her to um and ah. He wasn't going to cajole or try to convince her. This was a single offer and she had a single second to decide.

She nodded.

'Follow my lead.' He let her go and turned towards the stairs. 'No matter what.'

Back up on deck Jasper was standing with his briefcase in hand. Her uncle was attempting to hide his anger and disappointment by talking incessantly about the tourism boom. Zara stood terrified at a distance, knowing her uncle would be even angrier that she'd returned to the deck.

'Sit back down, Jasper,' Tomas said with deceptive softness. 'I've had some time to think about things some more while freshening up.'

'You have?' The glow of bitterness in her uncle's eyes morphed to avaricious excitement. 'Go fetch more drinks, Zara. Now.'

'No, I want her to stay,' Tomas overruled him firmly. 'She's a crucial detail to this possible deal.'

Cold sweat slid down Zara's spine. Surely he wouldn't call her uncle out for hitting her? She sent Tomas a desperate look, but he wasn't looking at her at all.

'I want your niece,' Tomas said bluntly. 'I'll invest in your casino operations, but only if I have Zara.'

Zara's heart stopped. She couldn't have heard right.

'You want Zara?' Her uncle narrowed his eyes. 'You can't want—'

'Those are my terms.' Tomas didn't let her uncle continue. 'Without Zara there will be no investment.'

'You want...' Her uncle just stared at him in shock. 'How do I know you're serious?'

'I'll marry her,' Tomas answered bluntly. 'How soon can we arrange that, Jasper?'

It took five seconds for Charles to collect himself and shut his dropped jaw.

Terrified, she stared from Tomas to Charles to Jasper. The lawyer's face was utterly impassive while he checked data on his tablet, as if his boss made outrageous queries every day. He'd said to follow his lead, but this was almost barbaric.

'It seems...er...that you can marry today if you really want to,' Jasper said, sending his boss a covert look. 'There's no notice or stand-down period required. Just the fee, two witnesses and passports.'

'Good,' Tomas said, ignoring that warning plea in the tone from his lawyer. 'So we can leave now.'

Zara stared at her uncle, trying to read his reaction. Surely he'd say no to such a preposterous suggestion? Surely he'd have some compunction?

But a greedy light entered his eye. 'You'll be my nephew-in-law.'

'That's right.' Tomas nodded. 'We'll be family.'

A prickle ran down Zara's spine at something in Tomas's tone. There was something so very cold when he said that word.

Uncle Charles smiled. 'She can cook.' He nodded, as if suddenly approving of her skills. 'She's a virgin too, you know.' His proud smile made her skin crawl. 'She's been very sheltered.'

She closed her eyes, engulfed in scalding shame and mortification. He was talking about her as if she were a thing to be traded. And as if her sexual experience were anything that mattered?

'Then it's decided. Zara, go pack your bag.' Tomas issued the order without even looking at her.

Sickened to her soul, she knew she had no choice. If she stayed she'd be her uncle's skivvy and, increasingly, his punchbag, for the foreseeable future. His temper would

*only worsen the more his business failed. And now she
knew how he really saw her. How he'd trade her for some
stupid business deal.*

*'Wait.' A suspicious twist tightened her uncle's mouth.
'I'll come with you to the register office.'*

*'Of course,' Tomas said unblinkingly, staring her uncle
down. 'You'll want to witness the wedding. Go and pack
now, Zara.'*

*Her uncle hadn't even bothered to ask her how she felt
about it. He was acting as if he owned her. But then, that
was how he'd always acted. She meant absolutely nothing
to him. She'd been a source of money—and when that had
gone, she'd become little more than another of his staff.
Only he hadn't had to pay her.*

She left the room without a word. And then she ran.

Zara poured steaming-hot chocolate into two mugs and
blinked back the tears at the recollection of how little her
uncle had cared for her. But she was away from him now—
and so much stronger.

She sprinkled a hint of cinnamon on the top of each.
She found a half-empty packet of biscuits at the back of
the cupboard and added a few to a small plate and loaded
the wooden tray she found in a cupboard.

It had all happened so quickly it was almost a blur. Yet
those moments were seared in her mind. There she'd stood
in the council offices shivering in a cheap sundress and
make-up covering the mark from where her uncle had hit
her.

The ceremony had been ridiculously brief. Uncle Charles
had witnessed it. Jasper had been the other signatory and
given Tomas a ring to slide onto her frozen finger. Heaven
knew where he'd found it so quickly.

She could have said no. She could have tried to tell the

officials that it was all a farce and that her uncle was insisting she marry a stranger. But she didn't. She'd just said yes.

There'd been no photos. No glasses of champagne. No speeches. And no kiss. Tomas had given her a cool peck on her cheek when the official had given the corny 'you may kiss the bride' permission. She'd pushed away that fleeting feeling of disappointment, reminding herself it wasn't real.

Her uncle had stood practically rubbing his hands in glee as she married the wealthiest man either of them had ever met. But Tomas Gallo had flipped the tables on Uncle Charles completely. He'd waited until they returned her uncle to the marina before dropping the bomb. He'd told her to remain in the car, but she'd opened her door already and could hear every word between the two men now eyeballing each other.

'I've changed my mind about the deal,' Tomas said coolly. 'I'm not going to buy into your company.'

'But you just—'

'We signed nothing and there was no formal agreement,' Tomas continued, ignoring the interruption. 'Jasper, Zara and I are leaving now and you won't see us again.'

'You...you...'

For the first time she saw her uncle lost for words. Suddenly he spun towards her, his face contorted with rage.

'You manipulative little...' He lunged for her through the open car door but Tomas stepped in front of her like an avenging angel.

'She's my wife.' Tomas bit the words out. 'And you'll leave her alone.'

'Your wife? She's worse than useless. She won't be—'

'I neither want nor expect anything from her,' Tomas interrupted, still ice-cold. 'She's not a commodity to me.'

He jerked his head at Jasper and the lawyer closed

the car door, sealing her away from the ugliness and the threats. But she could still hear their conversation.

'Try to contact her again and I will destroy the little you have left of a life.'

She shivered at the ruthless promise.

Her uncle fell back a step. 'You can't destroy me. I'll go to the media—'

'And tell them you sold your niece to a total stranger? The same girl who bears the bruises from your fist?' Tomas coolly goaded. 'You're a gambling man. You know it's time to cut your losses and leave.'

Tomas got back into the car and drove them away. The last time she saw her uncle he was red-faced, sweaty and defeated.

Tomas's mouth was held firm and she didn't dare speak a word as he drove them away from her uncle and towards the hotel he was staying in. She could feel the cold rage rolling off him. Jasper, sitting in the back seat, was utterly mute.

Tomas glanced at her and suddenly broke the silence. 'Don't be frightened. He won't bother you again.'

She was still afraid. She had no idea what she was going to do.

'You'll fly to London in the morning,' Tomas continued, turning his attention back to the road. 'I have your passport from your uncle as we needed it for the wedding. Jasper will ensure the marriage is annulled in the next few days. I will gift you a one-off payment. You never have to return here and you never have to see him again. Or me, for that matter. You're free to do as you wish.'

Her fears melted away. She bit her lip. She didn't know how to thank this man. She couldn't even look him in the eyes; he was so gorgeous, and now he'd done this?

'Your uncle is a greedy gambler and poor businessman. He thought our marriage would mean I'd committed to his

company. He didn't bother asking me to draw up any bind-
ing documents in regards to any investment. He thought
he'd won the lottery and showed just what he was capable
of.' He shook his head regretfully. 'He thought he could sell
you.' He pulled up outside the hotel and sent her a small
smile. 'But we got him, didn't we?'

He was so handsome and, in that moment, almost mis-
chievous...

On a whim she'd probably never fully understand, he'd offered her an escape and she'd sold herself to him that very
afternoon.

But he'd never actually wanted *her*. He was too much the
maverick for that. It was his distaste for her uncle that had
forced him to act. In less than forty-eight hours Tomas had
gotten her out of there and then disappeared from her life.

She lifted the tray and made herself lift her chin. She did
owe him. And now it seemed she was going to owe him for
yet more—a night's accommodation to wait out the storm.

As she walked back along the corridor and headed up
the wide staircase, she realised his wing of the house was
warm. The luxurious thick carpet was plush and intricate.
It truly was a stately home with its antique furniture and
polished wood. On the first floor she glanced at the walls,
expecting gilt-edged frames of the family portrait gallery.

That was when she paused in amazement. There were
pictures, but they weren't in frames. Slowly she progressed
along the gallery towards the lit room at the end that she
assumed was his office. But she was unable to look away
from the pages and pages pinned to the wall. Pictures of
people with notes written underneath all of them—dates,
times, messages about meetings, details about the indi-
viduals pictured.

Her heart pounded. It was like the case room in some

FBI movie. Was she in a house with a total psychopath or was he some kind of overachieving stalker?

Of course he wasn't. She knew that about him. She knew he was ruthless, yes. But he was also kind. And he was ferociously good at his job.

She looked again and saw there was a rough timeline to the wall. It covered almost a decade. There were pictures of Tomas as well and hand-scrawled notes in pencil beneath. Press clippings about himself as if he were a total narcissist? It just didn't make sense.

A horrible feeling sank into her bones. All these people pictured were people connected to him, mostly through business. They were people he knew.

Or *had* known.

She replayed that conversation they'd had only minutes ago on his doorstep—remembering his abruptness, his defensiveness. And when he'd asked that question—*'Do I know you?'*

He hadn't looked angered as much as guarded. He hadn't wanted to ask her that question. What had he been wary of? Her answering *yes*?

Why would that have been a problem? Because he hadn't remembered her?

If he'd asked 'have we met?' she wouldn't have lied. But she'd hidden behind semantics. Now she registered that there was more than an arrogant aloofness to him, there was a barrier. He was locked away. She remembered Jasper's agitation and insistence that Tomas was still suffering since that accident. Her own hurt pride had blinded her to the obvious.

She knew Tomas had carried Jasper to safety seconds before the car had exploded—that had been well documented in the press. It had been reported that Tomas had been thrown to the ground with his leg shredded. And his head?

He didn't welcome guests, didn't want intrusion. Why? Because he didn't want to talk about anyone, or himself?

She feared there was a very good reason for that and she was furious with Jasper for not telling her the truth. What else hadn't he told her?

'What are you doing in here?'

She jumped at the furious demand and almost dropped the tray she was carrying. Turning, she saw Tomas had come up behind her. The iciness in his eyes was impenetrable. He was *livid*.

Her blood quickened. 'Looking for you.'

But the plush carpet had masked his footfall.

'You do not come up here. *Ever,*' he snapped.

Zara's anger flared—a mixture of guilt and outrage. He was rude and arrogant and she didn't care how much of a hard time he'd had, there was no need to be so vile to someone. She'd been spoken to like that too many times in her life and she no longer stood for it. *Ever.* 'No wonder you can't keep staff when you speak to them like that.'

He visibly recoiled and then blinked. 'The Kilpatricks have been loyal to me all this last year. They're only away this weekend to attend a family celebration.'

She gaped at him for a second. 'That wasn't what I was told.'

'And what were you told exactly?' He stepped forward and grasped her shoulders. 'And by whom?'

'I told you. Jasper. He said you'd been left without any staff. That you needed someone for a week or so.'

'How do you know him?'

'I told you that already too. He helped me out a while back.'

'Helped you out?'

She threw him a look as she heard the insinuation in his tone. 'He's old enough to be my father.'

'That doesn't stop many women. He's very wealthy—'

'You just can't stop insulting me, can you?' She glared at him. 'I'm here to help you, because your friend asked me to come. If you have an issue with it, take it up with him.'

'I intend to.'

Biting her lip, she glanced at the wall again. She couldn't help it. And the thing was, she had taken *Tomas's* money.

But that was partly why she was here. To make amends and show her gratitude. Only now did she realise just how impossible that might be.

'Don't ask,' he said shortly as he followed the line of her sight to the picture-strewn walls.

'I wasn't going to.'

Because now she thought she understood. Her anger melted as her heart broke for him. She was so very sorry. 'This part of the house is cosy.'

'I've put the heating on in your room.' His expression became remote and he released her to step away. 'And in the kitchen. It should be better in a few more minutes. The whole house temperature is controlled to protect the art and furnishings that are in storage. I'm not into wasting resources.'

Tomas watched as Zara nodded and placed the tray she was carrying onto a nearby low table. She lifted up one of the mugs. He refused to be tempted but he could smell the chocolate. He hadn't had chocolate in a long, long time.

But when she turned back, Tomas read pity in her eyes and it infuriated him. 'Still think I can't cope alone?' he asked bitterly.

'I don't think that,' she said briefly. 'Jasper was the one worrying. He said you're likely to work so hard you'd forget to eat. That you won't bother taking the time to cook yourself something decent. And it's not like you can get a pizza delivery tonight.'

For some reason the thought of Jasper talking about him with her got right under his skin. His right-hand man had always had affairs with beautiful women. Young and old. But with Zara? It didn't gel. And it hadn't happened. She didn't need to tell him again.

Now her small smile returned and it mollified him.

'So here you are,' he muttered. Like a temptress.

'Would you like some hot chocolate?' She held out the mug to him. 'That's why I came up here.'

Slowly he shook his head. 'I don't eat sugar.'

'You're diabetic?' She frowned and clasped the mug back close to her with her other hand. 'Any other dietary requirement I should know about?'

'I'm not diabetic. I simply prefer not to eat too much sugar.' He wanted to get back to peak physical health.

'Maybe you should, it might sweeten you up,' she mumbled as she turned away about to return downstairs.

'What was that?' Her attitude took him by surprise. She was like a little spitting kitten with not very sharp claws but she wasn't afraid to give him a swipe.

'No sugar. Got it.' She turned back and smiled brightly at him. That dimple appeared.

Her small show of fearlessness amused him. He almost smiled back.

'It's not good for my recovery,' he explained reluctantly, because he didn't want her to walk away just yet. That smile was bewitching.

A small frown pleated her brow as she looked him over—but her checking for his recovery took a twist. Her expression changed and a dazed look entered her eyes, colour ran up under her cheeks. Tomas tensed at her undeniable sensual awareness of him and he couldn't resist another assessment of his own.

She'd taken off that almost useless rain jacket, revealing she wore only a thin T-shirt underneath. The curves in those jeans were not girlish in any way; frankly they were generous. The sneakers didn't help her in the height department at all and when he'd held her from him just before he'd felt the slenderness of her shoulders. The sheer femininity of her made him catch his breath. It had taken every ounce of will to refrain from sliding his hand to her narrow waist and pulling her flush against him. He ached to feel those soft curves against him.

Hell, he'd turned into a pervert in two minutes flat.

She gulped at the hot chocolate as if she needed to do something with herself. He watched as she swallowed it back. The scent of the warm liquid assailed his senses. It was the first time in ages he'd regarded food as anything other than fuel. He looked at the speck of creamy milk left on her lip and his mouth watered.

'Are you sure you don't want some?' Her eyes were wide and her voice a mere whisper.

Any other woman and he'd have thought it was a come-on, but the candour in those eyes spoke volumes.

He ought to tell her that she'd left a bit of chocolate milky foam on her lip, but he wasn't going to. Too much of a cliché. He would not notice. He was well practised at eliminating extraneous thoughts from his mind. All that mattered was his work and rebuilding his company into something better than before the accident that had almost destroyed him.

No one would ever know how bad his injuries had been or the degree to which he'd suffered. The public perception of him—the belief in his knowledge and skill—needed to be unshakeable. Because he was his company.

No one could ever know the truth. He could never allow himself to be that exposed.

As he silently regarded her, her pupils grew and that sweet colour deepened in her cheeks as she realised the *double entendre* she'd inadvertently uttered. She caught her lip with her teeth. And then—to his surprise—she smiled again.

Grimly he stared at her, unable to speak. He wanted to kiss her—taste that smile and the sweetness deep inside her.

'Tomas?' Her voice was the thinnest of whispers now and uncertainty had stolen into her expression as she looked into his face.

No, she wasn't one of Jasper's ladies of pleasure. She was too confused by this undeniable electricity that arced whenever they so much as glanced at each other. But she couldn't help the way she looked at him or hide the hazy desire evident in her eyes and in the way her breathing quickened the nearer he got to her.

She was as thrown as he. Only Tomas was a master of hiding everything now.

But the temptation was almost too great.

'I'll get your bag from the car,' he said abruptly.

'I'll go tidy the kitchen.' She turned and all but ran from him.

He watched her go.

No, he wasn't doing anything about this sexual attraction no matter how intense. He didn't have the time or the desire to fool around. And he couldn't risk exposure.

Except all he could think about were her curves. And her mouth. And the irrepressible sparkles in her eyes. She was like a sensual pixie specially sent to torment him.

Damn Jasper.

CHAPTER THREE

'You can't sleep?'

ZARA WAS STILL trembling when she made her way to the kitchen. She'd been so overwhelmed by the desire to kiss him, she'd almost leaned into him. But she'd mistaken that look in his eyes, because he'd then looked so forbidding. She'd almost humiliated herself all over again.

She fished her phone out of her bag, frowning at the low number of battery bars. She needed to charge it soon. Before anything, though, she needed to talk to Jasper.

She hit him with it the second he answered. 'Why didn't you tell me the truth?'

'Zara?'

At his sharp reply her bravado faded. 'Why didn't you tell me about Tomas?'

There was a pause. 'What did he say when he saw you?'

'He has no idea who I am.'

'He didn't recognise you?' Jasper's disappointment was more than audible; she felt it echoing over the ether.

'Why did you tell me his staff had walked out on him?' she asked plaintively. 'You lied to me. You set me up.'

'I thought it might work,' he answered a touch belligerently. 'It was my last—'

'What might work?'

'That he'd see you again and…'

She waited. Then she guessed anyway. 'You hoped he'd remember me.'

'Zara.'

'That's what you meant, isn't it? When you said he had injuries, you meant his memory. Because there isn't anything else. He's very…fit.' She drew in a shuddering breath and leaned against the kitchen counter. 'I'm right, aren't I? He's lost his memory.' She waited for his reply. 'Jasper?'

'I can't tell you. I promised him.'

'I'm different.' She wasn't just anyone. She'd been the man's wife.

'No. Not even you,' Jasper muttered, sounding older than his years. 'He saved my life too, you know.'

'Jasper—'

'He needs help.' Jasper suddenly interrupted her. 'He's not left that house all year. All he does is work—'

'He doesn't need *my* help. He needs professional help.' She wasn't a professional *anything*. She blinked back the tears as she whispered, 'I'm not the right person. He deserves better than this.' He deserved better than her.

Jasper had been wrong in setting them both up like this. He'd lied to Tomas and made her an accessory. She hated that.

The phone cut out a couple of times and she guessed someone else was trying to phone Jasper, but he ignored it.

She thought of that lonely gallery up there with Tomas's life in pictures and articles on the wall. The notes he had and what must be a desperate attempt to make sense of it all. 'Can he remember anything?'

'I can't talk about it, Zara. I promised him I wouldn't. But he's lost so much. You can see how isolated he is. I thought if he just saw you…'

But she'd been nothing in Tomas's life—only a moment, a whimsy. She hadn't truly touched him or made any lasting impression on him. He'd turned her world upside down, then walked away without so much as a backwards glance. All done in a little over a day.

She'd meant nothing to him.

'I can't stay here,' she said. Jasper had trapped her in

a situation she'd never have agreed to had she known the truth.

'You must,' Jasper said firmly. 'It will take a couple of days until I get there. Work as his housekeeper. I can get him to agree to that.'

'No—'

'You can't leave, Zara.' He overrode her.

'Why not?'

There was a hesitation, then a sigh. 'Because you're still married to him.'

'What?' Every muscle in her body weakened and she almost dropped the phone. *'What?'*

'You're still married. The annulment was never processed. I'm sorry.'

She was still married to Tomas? Goosebumps skittled over her skin. She drew in a breath so jagged it seemed to slice her lungs. 'How is that possible?' she whispered.

'After the accident, I was so distracted it slipped my mind.'

'But the paperwork… I signed—' She broke off, too stunned to speak.

'It burned in the car. We were in hospital for weeks. Tomas was there for months. Then I was concerned about him—protecting him.'

She'd read in the newspaper about the car accident in France less than a week after their crazy wedding. She'd felt sick at the time as she'd learned how Tomas had fought to get Jasper free of the wreckage before the car had exploded. But they'd both survived the accident and the blast and, according to the reports, both were going to be fine. There'd been little about the man in his bio on his business website. Other online searches had been business related and largely fruitless.

Not long after that that she'd forced herself to stop searching for information on him. She couldn't turn into some sad obsessive. She'd had to forget him to move forward with her life. But her repayment plan had always burned in the background. In the long term she'd aimed to track him down, successful, a whole new woman. With the money plus interest to return to him. She'd wanted to impress him with her transformation and her success.

She'd never do that now.

'No one knows?' She turned and stared at the dark window but she could see nothing but her own pale face in the glass.

'No one knows anything about you. Only his medical team know about...'

She felt the ground had been cut out from under her. All this time they'd been married? And all these months he'd been so *hurt*?

'You're coming here now, aren't you? Please,' she begged. She couldn't handle this alone. 'He has to know,' she said, her old anxiety rushing to the fore. She should go in there right now and tell him, but she couldn't do it. More than that, he wouldn't believe her. She had no proof. He'd think she was crazy. And she wouldn't blame him. 'Please, you have to tell him...'

She didn't want to do more harm than good. She didn't want to make anything worse for him. And she didn't want him to know how weak she'd been.

Truth?

She was still weak. And she was still half in love with him.

She heard the series of interruptions signalling Jasper was getting another call, but again he ignored it.

'We both owe him, Zara.'

She closed her eyes against the emotional manipulation. So many times that had been used against her. But this time was different. Because this time she *did* owe.

Tomas. *Everything.*

'I know,' she said softly.

'Stay until I get there.'

'Yes,' she agreed. Defeated.

'Is that Jasper you're talking to?'

She jumped at the question that cracked across the room like a bullwhip. Tomas stood in the kitchen doorway, looking furious, his own mobile phone in his hand. How long had he been standing there? What had he heard?

Then it hit her. She was staring at her *husband*.

'Zara?'

She didn't answer Jasper's sharp query because in two steps Tomas was across the room and had snatched the phone from her limp fingers.

'*Never* ignore my calls,' he said furiously into her phone to Jasper, not taking his eyes off her.

She heard Jasper's immediate reply. She hadn't got that apologetic deferential tone from him. The grim look on Tomas's face deepened as Jasper muttered something else she couldn't hear because now her mind whirled at the implication of Jasper's words.

She was still married to Tomas. She was his *wife*. She quivered as a frisson of intimacy that she had no right to feel skittered down her spine.

She'd always been too aware of him, too attracted, too ready to say yes.

Now she was here in this huge house alone with him and while he might have no clue about the truth, that didn't mean he wasn't totally, utterly in control.

And she wasn't. Not of herself. Not of those stupid yearnings she'd felt when he—and only he—was near. She'd been too isolated. Too inexperienced. Too insecure.

She licked her lips nervously as she watched his anger flare at Jasper.

At totally the wrong moment that one precious memory slipped its leash to torment her.

* * *

'You can't sleep?'

She shook her head, feeling her colour mount because he'd found her awake and alone at two in the morning, pacing the corridor outside her hotel room like an undead wraith unable to rest. She stopped outside her door, her bare toes curling into the carpet, and half hoped he'd just pass by and leave her to her own agony.

She had the most massive crush on him. How could she not? He was gorgeous and kind and mesmerising. And he'd helped her.

She knew the crush was mostly gratitude—she was confusing desire with appreciation. Their wedding that afternoon wasn't real in any way. He'd said it would be annulled in a couple of days once she was safely back in England. So this awareness of him could just die a death.

'And you're a bit scared?' Tomas asked with a gentle smile. 'I remember when I left Italy with nothing but the clothes I was wearing, I was scared, but it was an adventure.'

Her surprise grew; he'd become this successful from absolutely nothing? 'How did you make it?'

'Hard work. Determination.' He shrugged as he stepped closer until he was right in front of her. 'You have skills, you have more resources than you know. You're going to be fine.' He tilted her chin and looked into her eyes with a small smile. 'And your uncle was wrong, you know. You're very attractive.'

His lips brushed hers in the lightest gesture of support— and finality.

She screwed her eyes shut, her humiliation total. Her first ever kiss had come from her first lethal crush, and it had been born of compassion.

'Please don't pity me,' she muttered, then forced herself to look at him. 'I am going to be fine.' She echoed his

words, drawing strength from them. Determined to believe they would be the truth.

His eyes were only millimetres from hers, bottomless, unreadable, so beautiful and for a timeless moment all she could do was drown in them.

'I know,' he answered, his voice suddenly roughened.

And to her surprise, he quickly bent and brushed his lips over hers ever so lightly again. Without volition she parted her lips, lifting her chin so the sweet contact lingered just for a fraction longer. She closed her eyes to hold onto the magic. And then everything changed.

He was back, his mouth moving over hers more firmly. Then more so again. She quivered, stifling a gasp when his tongue slid between her teeth, searching out her secrets. It felt foreign, but it felt so good as he stroked her that she simply leaned into him.

She heard a low growl in the back of his throat as his arms came around her. He kissed her again. She opened more for him; she couldn't not. And she sought the same knowledge, darting her tongue to tangle with his, to push past and explore him. A wave of emotion rose in her, tearing apart the veneer of fear and releasing an intense desire that had never before been roused. It was so raw and new she had no hope of either containing or controlling it. Instinctively she knew that her response inflamed him too— the kiss grew more passionate. She wound her arms around his neck, curling her fingers in the hair at the back of his neck. Her action bringing her body into full contact with his—her breasts pressed against his hard chest. Spasms of awareness shot from her taut nipples to the depths of her most private parts. It was shocking and delightful all at once and she simply didn't know what to do other than press closer and closer still.

This wasn't gratitude. This wasn't anything as easy as that. This was a desperate meeting of two spirits that had suddenly curled together and couldn't be forced apart. She moaned as that fire inside built to an unbearable temperature. She needed something more...

But all of a sudden he wrenched his lips from hers. She gasped in disappointment, but then clamped her mouth shut as embarrassment crashed down on her.

There was an unreadable expression in his eyes as he pulled her arms from where she'd wound them round his neck. She had to lean back against the wall for support as he put three feet of distance between them.

Oh, Lord, she'd been clinging to him. She closed her eyes tightly to hide from him. She wanted to apologise but she couldn't. She was trembling too much to summon coherent speech.

She heard the sound of her hotel-room door opening and she opened her eyes in a flash. But he'd stepped back from it and wasn't looking at her as he crisply ordered her to bed.

'You'd better try to sleep now, you have a long journey tomorrow.'

Alone.

As if she could ever sleep after that. Her husband had kissed her—meaning nothing but a little comfort—but she'd succumbed so totally, tumbling into a heady fantasy of fate.

That fantasy had been hers alone. He'd almost wordlessly walked away, unable to even look at her. And her humiliation was complete all over again.

She closed her eyes briefly now to force the burning memory back into its padlocked box. And she bit down on her lip to stop that pulse of desire tormenting her.

Not now. Not ever.

He'd never been hers in that way. And now he never could be.

* * *

Tomas gripped Zara's phone, his annoyance burning brighter as he looked at how pale she now was. What had Jasper been saying to her?

There was an almost beseeching look in her sea-green eyes, as if she was wordlessly asking for something. Asking for—

He didn't want to know what it was. He could never give her it anyway.

He had nothing to give anyone.

But now he had a woman before him looking so damnably beautiful. And alone. Looking as if she needed comfort. And contact. And—

He turned on his heel and stalked out of the kitchen.

'Leave your playgirls in London,' he growled in a low voice. 'I have too much to do for this distraction.'

'You always have too much to do and not all distractions are bad,' Jasper tried to joke.

But Tomas wasn't in the mood. 'Why did you send her to me?' he barked as he braved the rain to get her bag from the car. The car was cheap and not in the best condition and he was surprised it had got her here safely. Her bag wasn't heavy; she obviously hadn't planned to stay long.

'Because you shouldn't be alone for weeks at a time.'

Tomas snorted. Being alone was exactly how he liked it. As it was he hadn't been going to be alone for long enough. 'The Kilpatricks will be back next week.'

'You don't exactly let them into your life.'

Tomas paused. How did Jasper know that? Did he get them to report to him? He was livid at the intrusion—well-intentioned or not. 'Don't interfere, Jasper. Work is all that matters.'

'Haven't you proved that already?' Jasper argued quietly. 'The company is more successful now than it ever has been. No one can believe the way you've pushed it on this last year…isn't it time you had a break and took care of other aspects of your life?'

'There are no other aspects,' Tomas snapped. 'And there never have been. You know it as well as I.' That was how he liked it and wanted it. 'I pay you for your legal advice and nothing more. If you want me to *keep* paying you, then I suggest you stick to the books.'

There was silence as Jasper digested that threat. 'I'm sorry. I shouldn't have…' He cleared his throat. 'But Zara is a good worker, please give her a chance for these few days. She needs it.'

Tomas closed his eyes at the plea in the older man's voice and blocked the memory of the anxiety in Zara's eyes. He'd known there was more to her story than what she'd told him.

And he knew Jasper had a habit of helping out stray dogs.

'She's been through all the checks?' He needed to know she could be discreet.

She suspected already; he'd seen it in her eyes as she'd looked at his gallery. It was exactly why he didn't want strangers in the house. And he sure as hell did not want her pity.

Anger coursed through his blood again.

'Of course.' Jasper sounded distracted.

'Where did you find her?' Tomas asked, not entirely believing him.

'The usual agency.'

'I don't need her.' Cait Kilpatrick had left enough meals to last him six months. Though, to be honest, he didn't like them.

Jasper's sigh came heavily down the phone. 'It's just for three or four days. She needs the money.'

'Then have her come and work for you,' Tomas said irritably. He hated being coerced. It was only because the old guy was so loyal that he'd let him. Because Jasper once helped him in a very similar way all those years ago. It was one of the last things Tomas could remember before it all went blank.

'Tom—'

'She can have the money and just leave,' Tomas said. She didn't need to stay and disrupt his solitude. He didn't want her here, making him think. Or wonder. Or want.

He only wanted to focus on his work.

'But she has pride,' Jasper said quietly. 'Not unlike you.'

Tomas gritted his teeth.

'The experience would be good for her,' Jasper added in a wheedling tone.

'You're saying she's inexperienced?' Tomas looked to the heavens in frustration. 'How do you know what would be so good for her if she was just from the agency—she's worked for you?' There was more to Jasper's story than he was letting on. What was it about Zara that was so important?

'For a short time, yes,' Jasper muttered.

Tomas knew Jasper was lying but he didn't know why. 'You really think I can't handle a few days all by myself?' he jeered.

'I think you can handle almost anything,' Jasper replied. 'You might even cope with her for a few days if you try hard enough.'

Tomas managed a laugh. But he wasn't so sure. He was staying out of her way.

That smile? Those brightly shining eyes? She was like a damn puppy, so eager to please and cheerful and, he suspected, in need of affection and attention.

He didn't have any of that to give.

'I'll come see you in a few days and make sure she hasn't poisoned you. I wouldn't blame her if she does if you're this grouchy with her.'

Was he grouchy? Probably. But then he had reason to be, didn't he? 'Come soon and take her away. I don't need her.'

And he refused to want her.

He walked back down to the kitchen. She stood staring out of the dark window but when she caught sight of his reflection over her shoulder she whirled to face him.

'What did he say to you?' he said as he held her phone out to her. His eyes narrowed as he saw how pale she still looked. How warily she ensured her fingers did not brush his again as she took her phone from him.

'He apologised.'

He almost smiled, surprised with her honesty. 'He did the same to me. You'll stay a few days and be my house-keeper.'

Her stiffness eased. 'Until he gets here.' She nodded, her lips twisting wryly. 'I'm sorry he foisted me on you.'

He couldn't help the small smile at that mental image. Did she really think it was Jasper who'd made the final call? 'I guess I'll get over it,' he muttered ironically.

Did she even have anywhere else to go?

But her dimple popped back as she returned his smile with that small one of her own. He was glad. But he was still damn uncomfortable.

'I'll be in my office most of the time,' he explained roughly. 'Working.'

'I promise I'll stay out of your way and only come to find you at mealtimes,' she said, a little too meekly.

He shot her a look. 'I will come to the kitchen.'

'Will you remember to?' A spark of mischief lit her eyes.

'Of course I will.'

Her brows flickered at his snap and her smile widened. 'Thank you.' Ultra-meek that time.

He drew in a steadying breath. She *was* an undaunted kitten. 'I'll show you to your room.'

Silently she walked alongside him as he led her back

up to his wing. It was the only one with the furnishings uncovered and ready for use. She had to stay too close for comfort.

He was too aware of how close she was now. How warm she looked with that flush back in her cheeks and the shine back in her eyes. She looked soft and the desire to pull her close was too intense.

Inwardly he cursed Jasper again.

'You'll sleep here.' He stopped by the open door and tried not to look at her. He failed. 'Don't be afraid to turn up the heater if it still isn't warm enough for you.'

He remembered too well how cold her fingers had been when she'd first arrived.

'Thank you,' she said, subdued. The light, sparring moment had passed and whatever thoughts she'd had before were troubling her anew. She avoided looking him in the eyes as she waited, clearly tense again.

He frowned, another wisp of *déjà vu* distracting him.

'I'm just along the corridor should you need anything.' He walked away abruptly, wondering how on earth he was ever going to sleep tonight.

CHAPTER FOUR

'He can afford this, you know, it doesn't mean anything to him.'

ZARA STEPPED INTO the vast room. Beautiful wood panelling lent warmth to it, as did the intricately patterned rug thrown over the thick carpet. Antique furniture gleamed in the soft light from the table lamp—a pair of plump armchairs sat at angles in front of the small fire, a polished free-standing mirror reflected the grandeur of the room, while dominating the lot was the large four-poster bed with its beautiful moss-green and gold brocade coverings. Heavy-looking curtains were drawn over the windows, blocking out the wild weather and adding to the air of luxurious sanctuary. She felt as if she'd walked onto the set of a sumptuous period drama and the effect was spellbinding.

She toed off her cold shoes and stepped towards the gently flickering flames in the decoratively tiled fireplace. But the fire was more for ambience than heat, for there was hidden modernisation—a discreet switch that allowed her to control the temperature with the touch of a button. Through an open doorway she saw an en suite bathroom with gleaming porcelain and fluffy white towels.

Her bag was on the low wooden luggage rack and she opened it, hunting for the winter pyjamas she'd thrown in there. Then she showered, her body slowly warming at last under the strong stream of steaming water.

She still couldn't believe any of it—that she was here, that he'd lost so much.

That he was still her *husband*.

She stepped out of the shower, wrapping herself in the

thick towel as she shivered again, unwilling to let herself think too closely about that. He wasn't *really* her husband. There wasn't any intimacy at all between them.

No matter what that rogue part of her might want.

Dressed in her nightwear, she walked towards the large bed, hyper aware of the tiny, muted sounds coming from somewhere in the house. The last time they'd slept under the same roof they'd been in that hotel on Antigua before she'd returned to England for the first time in ten years.

'Ready to go, Zara?'

Tomas's quick glance was keen as he met her in the hotel restaurant to take her directly to the airport, but then he looked at his watch as if he was impatient for them to go. For her to leave.

'Yes, thank you.' She knew she looked pale.

But he looked a touch paler to her eyes too.

'You have all you need?'

'Thank you for everything,' she offered quietly once he'd escorted her to the departure gate.

Words weren't enough. Nothing would ever be enough.

'Thanks are not necessary.' For just a second he hesitated. Her heart fluttered with the hope he might say for her to go with him instead. Or that he'd say he'd meet up with her in England. Or that he might kiss her again.

But he did none of those things. He stepped back. 'Go well.'

As she got to the corner of the air bridge she glanced back, but he'd already turned and was walking back through the busy airport.

It was over.

She'd spent the entire flight to London terrified she'd get turned back at Customs or something. But she hadn't been. She'd made her way north—choosing to go away from where her parents had lived because she never wanted her uncle to find her. She'd changed her surname for that reason too. She'd found a cheap bedsit near the centre of the town. That dream of studying *patisserie* in Paris had faded to the realistic aim of working in a café while studying at the local technical institute. Alone and with the resources to become fully independent.

Finally. And only thanks to Tomas.

But she'd wanted to use as little as necessary of his money because since that kiss, and their too-brief conversations, he'd become something more to her than just a source of escape.

Pushing away the painful memories, she curled up in the vast bed with its rich coverlets and luxury sheets. She didn't think she'd ever fall asleep, she was too wired. But sleep came—shockingly sudden and deep.

She had no idea of the time when she woke. She quickly got out of bed and pulled back the curtains to see how light it was and what the day was like.

The rain had stopped but the sky was covered in purplish, snow-heavy clouds. The world seemed eerily still as if on pause, waiting for the weather bomb. The clouds threatened that the worst was yet to come.

As she looked from the sky to the ground, the magnificence of her bedroom paled as she took in the marvel that was outlaid before her. Now she understood what Tomas had meant when he'd said the gardens had been closed to the public, for even in the heart of winter these were show gardens.

With a high brick wall around the perimeter, immaculate rows of precise hedges divided the garden into four separate formal 'rooms'—each decorated with fountains and immaculately patterned beds that even in this desolate weather were verdant and beautiful. And in the centre of the four sections stood the masterpiece—a perfectly maintained Victorian glasshouse. A third of the size of the manor itself, it was constructed of pristine white-painted ironwork and a myriad of gleaming windows through which she could see deep green exotic foliage. The whole vista was a beautiful, bountiful secret that only those in the manor—or those invited—would see.

It was a shame they were no longer open for people to enjoy because they were incredible. And someone maintained them to this perfection.

As she gazed in awe Tomas stepped out of the glasshouse into the centre of garden.

Zara froze, unable to stop herself staring. He wore shorts and a thin T-shirt and running trainers. Even from this distance she could see the jagged marks on his thigh. It had to have been a horrendous injury to have left such scarring, yet he had a barely noticeable limp. That was down to his sheer determination, she was sure. He'd clearly been working out—and by the look of him, he did that every day.

What other injuries had he worked hard to overcome? And what of his memory? Was his amnesia complete or did he have some memories still? Would those he'd lost ever return?

'Why did you do this?'

She'd finally got the courage to ask Tomas when Jasper had got out of the car to arrange the hotel room just after they'd left her uncle at the marina.

He'd helped her. He didn't have to. He could have just walked away leaving her uncle to fester in his own failure, leaving her there to cope with whatever onslaught and repercussions the man dealt. People turned a blind eye all the time. But Tomas had chosen to take action. He'd married her.

He sighed and turned in his seat to look at her directly.
'I dislike bullies.'
He gazed intently at her.

'You do understand there's nothing I want from you? I know what it's like to feel trapped.'

Silently she stared back at him.

'And I know what it's like not to be wanted.'

Tears burned her eyes but she couldn't blink. She couldn't tear her gaze from him...not even for a tenth of a second.

For that endless moment she'd looked just as intently back at him and she swore she'd glimpsed a once lonely youth beneath that confident, driven exterior.

Everyone had a past, everyone had hurts and suddenly she'd known that he'd done what he had because he'd been there himself. Abandoned. Afraid. Alone. The flash of insight hurt.

'We should get inside.'

He'd turned away from her. The moment had been broken.

She stared—here he was now, back from broken. But still wounded? He'd clearly fought so hard.

Her mouth dried as she got sidetracked by the visual of just how strong he was. There wasn't an ounce of fat on him, only a sheen of sweat over his skin, emphasising the defined muscled beneath. She'd never seen him so exposed and he was more gorgeous than she'd ever imagined. Unthinking, she inched closer to the window.

He looked up. For a second her gaze clashed with his—even from this distance she felt the burn in his eyes. Embarrassed, she stepped back, her skin all but blistering from being caught—*ogling* like some immature fangirl.

When she finally made it down to the kitchen twenty minutes later, he was already there. He'd showered and dressed in jeans and T-shirt and looked outrageously handsome with his hair still damp and his jaw unshaven.

That hot accusation in his eyes was still there too.

She tried to dodge it—hoping she could breeze through her embarrassment and that he hadn't read the raw attraction in her own eyes—by adopting a smile and avoiding meeting his gaze. 'What can I make you for breakfast?' she asked.

'I've already eaten,' he answered brusquely, turning his back to her.

Her smile became fixed. Of course he had. 'A drink, then—tea? Coffee?'

He shook his head.

'Then what would you like for lunch?' she asked, determined not to let his mood destroy her own.

He shrugged.

'You have no preference?' she persisted. 'None at all?'

'No.'

She rolled her eyes. 'Tomas, help me out a little. I'm only trying to do my job.'

'Cook whatever you want and I'll eat it. I have more important things to think about.'

'Good,' she snapped back. 'Go get on with that, then.' Suddenly she couldn't wait to get rid of him.

A startled expression flashed across his face but she could be tetchy too, if that was how he wanted it. And if he didn't want her cooking much for him that was fine too. She'd make what she enjoyed and he could eat it or not. The rest of the time she could test her recipes. She didn't exist purely to serve him, she had her own plans to be getting on with and his *you're here under my sufferance* attitude meant she now had some time to be getting on with them. And she wasn't going to feel guilty about it.

Even so, the first thing she did once he'd left was defrost one of the meals his housekeeper had left for him. She wrinkled her nose as she sampled it. While it was okay, she could see why he wasn't that enthused—nutritious but bland, it could do with some pep.

She surveyed the pantry again. There was no way she was going to be able to make anything decent without a trip to the shops. She was going to have to go to the nearest town and stock up.

Tomas sat at his desk and stared sightlessly at the screen. He couldn't muster any attention to read the reports that had landed in his inbox first thing. He'd been rude and he regretted it. Which annoyed him even more because she—and what she thought of him—shouldn't matter at all. But she'd worked her way under his skin already—and the way she looked at him?

It was exactly the way he tried *not* to look at her—with raw interest. That sensual awareness that was simply impossible. He had no need, time or desire for any kind of relationship. Not even the temporary, physical satisfaction kind.

He'd learned early on relationships weren't worth the risk—not if you wanted to survive and succeed. The only way to operate was alone. The only guarantee he had was his own.

He pulled out the thick leather-bound book that he always kept on his desk. The specialist had suggested he keep a daily journal but Tomas wasn't about to write about his 'feelings'. Rather he kept a record of each day's activities—his exercise regime, his reading, his work decisions and reasons.

If he lost more of his memory, he'd have that record as his reminder.

He'd had to retrain so much—had to read and concentrate round the clock to regain the confidence and knowledge he needed to lead his company again. He couldn't let anyone decimate his focus now. Especially not a young woman in a thin T-shirt and skinny jeans and an oversized apron. But last night was the first journal entry he'd missed in months. He didn't quite know how to classify Zara.

All he wanted to know was what she was doing right now.

It seemed his legendary focus was shot. Grimacing at his weakness, he pushed back his seat and quietly walked down to the kitchen.

She had her back to him as she leaned over the bench. He angled his head and saw she was rifling through a recipe book, but he was distracted from reading the title by her circling jeans-clad hips. He froze for a second, his tongue cleaved to the roof of his mouth as he watched the rhythmic undulations of those sweet curves. It took him a second to realise she had earbuds in and that she was partly dancing as she read. He zoned into the melodic strains leaking from the buds. It was familiar but he didn't recognise it. Of course he didn't.

'Zara?'

She didn't stop with the hip-circling.

'Zara.'

She jumped, gasping as she caught sight of him behind her.

'I didn't mean to startle you,' he said gruffly.

'I'm so sorry.' She hurriedly switched off the music on her phone.

'You don't need to apologise.' He frowned at how thrown she was by his appearance.

She coloured and her speech rushed. 'I didn't want to disturb you—you seem to like to work in silence.'

Only because he hadn't thought to put any music on. Maybe it would help. At the very least it would be something to break the silence and his wonderings about what *she* was doing.

'It's not good for your ears to wear earbuds all day,' he said. 'I don't mind if you play music using the sound system.' He gestured to the cupboard where the heating and media systems controls were.

'Really? You're sure?'

He frowned again, this time at how surprised and pleased she looked. Had he been that much of an ogre?

But now she'd recovered herself and that irrepressible smile appeared and he found he couldn't resist a reluctant tease.

'Of course.' He shot her a look. 'Just not too loud.'

He didn't miss the flash of her truly brilliant smile as he turned away. Feeling more at ease, he walked back up to his office, ready to restart his day.

Zara did a full reconnaissance of the garden and found a herb garden and vegetable plot hidden from the main vista. The produce was abundant but she needed other supplies. Clearly the housekeeper wasn't expecting Tomas to want to cook at all for himself given she'd left the pantry all but bare apart from the basics.

Deciding to brave his wrath, she walked up to his office, studiously not looking at the line-up of photographs and accompanying notes. The door was open so she knocked on the doorframe and tried not to stare too hard.

His office was a massive library—complete with roaring fire and bookcases lined with leather-bound classics, but there the period-drama set ended. Because he was seated at a desk in the centre of the room frowning at a screen full of numbers. A row of other computer screens were on the desk and switched on and showing markets informa-tion. A television was on mute but she saw it was switched to a twenty-four-hour news channel. Two phones were on the table beside him.

She knocked a second time.

'Yes?' He glanced at her.

This time she managed to bite back the automatic apol-ogy that sprang to her lips. She'd spent a decade doing nothing much but apologise—to her uncle for everything and anything. She'd never been able to do a thing right, a decade of not being or doing what he wanted.

She'd gone to him aged twelve—right in the middle of that rough phase of puberty with pimples and puppy fat and no confidence and grieving unbearably and his disappointment and disapproval only made it all worse.

But she'd done enough apologising in all that time. She'd learned to stop it now.

Well, almost.

But it was okay to interrupt Tomas. She was *helping* him. 'I'm going into the village to pick up some supplies. Is there anything in particular I can get you?'

'No.' He blinked at her. 'Thank you,' he added as an afterthought.

'What shops are there?' She risked a smile. 'Is there a good greengrocer?'

'I wouldn't know.' He turned back to the screen.

'You've not shopped there?'

'I don't go into the village.'

'You prefer London?' She waited, but got no answer. 'You don't go out much since your accident?'

Her first mention of the crash didn't impress him. 'It really is no concern of yours.'

Wasn't it? Wasn't it every concern of hers?

But he didn't know that yet. And she managed again not to apologise. Just.

'You'll need money.' He opened a drawer in the desk.

'I don't need that much,' she protested as she saw the roll of notes in his hand as he stood.

'Take it just in case.' He strolled over to give her the money.

'I'll go and investigate the shops, then.' She couldn't resist teasing a little. 'I might be a while.'

'Fine.' He headed back to his desk.

She shot him a look at his deliberately bland response.

'You won't change the security code at the gate while I'm gone?'

'So you're actually planning to come back?' he asked dryly.

'I promised Jasper I'd stay.' She tossed her head, pleased as his eyes narrowed in annoyance. 'I'm not afraid of a challenge. As long as you're not afraid to be honest.'

His eyebrows shot up and he took a step back towards her. 'What makes you think I wouldn't be honest?'

'Your desire to argue with me is too strong. Are you man enough to actually admit it if you like what I make for you?'

'Zara,' he said softly, a small smile playing about his lips. 'I've never been afraid to admit what I like.'

The innuendo was blatant—as was the look he directed from her top to toe, lingering in the middle.

Heat scorched her cheeks and his softly jeering laughter chased her from the room.

Her heart pounded and she touched her cold fingers to her hot lips. She knew he didn't mean it. He was just teasing; for a moment he'd been the Tomas she'd met that day— arrogant and decisive and with flashes of fun.

'Take care out there,' he suddenly called after her. 'The forecast isn't good.'

He was right about the weather. She'd barely got down the long driveway before light snow flurries began to fall. She wasn't worried—it wasn't too far to the village and she shouldn't be more than a couple of hours.

She walked the length of the picturesque main street, interested in the cafés and shops. She spent some time in each, looking at the artisan products they had on offer. There was a well-stocked general store and she browsed the aisles, stopping to read the notice board. A poster advertised the local farmers' market in the town square on the weekends.

'Can I help you?' a uniformed young assistant asked her.

'Is the market good?' Zara asked, gesturing to the poster.

The young woman nodded. 'It's in the town square, all year round. It's really good.' She smiled in a friendly way. 'Are you staying nearby?'

'Yes, at Raxworthy.' She mentioned the manor just to see the girl's reaction—if any.

It was instant. Her eyes widened in curiosity.

'At Raxworthy?' She was agog. 'With Tomas Gallo?' She looked eager for more information. 'You're working there?'

'For a few days,' Zara admitted briefly, now unable to avoid answering the question. Was it so obvious she wasn't there as a social guest? Of course it was.

She wasn't glamorous enough or well-dressed enough or anywhere near perfect enough to be anything other than the hired help.

No one would ever believe she was actually his wife.

That old unworthy feeling arose in her. She'd never been the confident social butterfly and her uncle's attempts to berate her into his ideal mould had failed.

Zara's only confidence had grown in the kitchen.

But while she was never going to be a society hostess type, that didn't mean she didn't have ambition. She knew what she wanted—her own business.

'So what's he like?' The young woman leaned forward, inviting confidence. 'We never see him. Is it true he's scarred?' Her voice dropped to a whisper. 'I've seen his picture on the Internet and he was so gorgeous. And so *wealthy...*'

'I really...couldn't say,' Zara answered weakly, regretting having said anything at all. She was aware the older woman standing nearby was listening intently.

Tomas was very private and Zara now understood why. She didn't blame him for keeping his distance from the village.

She paid for the groceries and put the bags into her car. The snow was falling heavily now and the visibility had reduced. But it was only a short drive.

Except five minutes into it her car made an appalling groaning sound, jerked and shuddered to a stop.

She pushed the accelerator to the floor but nothing happened. She tried the ignition a few more times—but still nothing happened. The fuel gauge showed there was quarter of a tank of petrol in it, which meant it was some kind of engine trouble.

Not something she had either the time or the money to deal with.

Worriedly, she got out of the car and looked up and down the quiet country lane. She couldn't leave her car in the middle of the road like this. She put it in gear and then tried to push it to the side of the road. She slipped and whacked her knee the first time. The second she got precisely nowhere. The third time the car began to inch forward. Pleased, she got a bout of energy and pushed harder, except the car then got away from her and slowly and gently crashed into the low wall at the edge of the road. The metal crunched.

Great. Just great.

Sighing, she fished her phone out of her bag only to stare at it in horror. It was totally out of charge. She'd forgotten to plug it in. She shook her head at her own uselessness. It didn't matter that she'd been so distracted last night, she should have remembered something so simple.

Now she had no choice but to walk. Fortunately she only had a few bags to carry and it wouldn't take more than another half-hour. No doubt Tomas would be appreciating the peace and quiet of having his big house to himself again.

She hoisted the bags in her hands, but then put them down again to double-check she had all the change to give back to him safely in her pocket. And she would give it all back to him.

* * *

'Why don't you want to take it all?'

Jasper looked stunned the morning after their wedding when she told him she didn't want to accept all the money Tomas had offered her the night before.

'He's done enough. I don't need all that amount. I only need enough to get started, and even then I'll pay that back. I want to pay him back as soon as I can.'

'He can afford this, you know,' Jasper said bluntly. 'It doesn't mean anything to him.'

'But it means something to me.'

Her heart ached as she remembered that kiss last night.

'Please,' she said quickly when she caught sight of the tall figure walking across the restaurant towards them. 'But I don't want him to know. Not yet.'

'Why not?' Jasper's smile was curious.

'He'll make me keep it.'

'Yes, he will.'

Jasper chuckled, but sobered just before Tomas came within earshot.

'Okay, but you must let me know your address once you're settled. You must let me know if you need anything more.'

She hadn't needed anything more. She'd *wanted*, but not needed.

Now she loaded up the shopping bags again and walked along the edge of the road, hoping any traffic would be able to see her. It was slow going as her sneakers had little tread and it was slippery on the fresh fallen snow. Her feet were wet already and her cheeks stinging from the cold and her hands sore from the heavy plastic bags.

Served her right for being so forgetful.

There was no traffic, almost no noise as the snow fell. All the sensible people would be safe indoors. Zara suddenly smiled to herself. So what? She was out in the snow and it might be cold but it was very beautiful and when she got back she could make hot chocolate and sit by the fire and try not to think about him—

'Zara! Zara!'

She stopped where she was on the side of the road, unwilling to believe either her ears or her eyes. But she recognised that tall figure materialising out of the white glare ahead of her. And she certainly recognised the abrupt tone of his voice as he furiously called out to her again as he saw her.

'Where the hell have you been?'

'To the village.' She swallowed. 'Remember?'

'What took you so long?' Tomas walked to within an inch of her personal space, looking slightly wild with his hair askew and fire in his eyes.

'I was getting what I needed.' Her voice went embarrassingly feeble.

Because he was staring at her, making the world shrink to those few inches between them. In this whitened world there was nothing but him any more.

'And what are you doing now?' he asked.

His implicit criticism galled her—firing her own anger. She didn't need him to judge. 'What do you think?'

'Why aren't you driving?'

She gritted her teeth and sent him a foul look.

'Where's your car?' he demanded.

'I'm not sure. It broke down back that way.'

Impossible as it ought to have been, he looked even more furious. 'Why didn't you phone me?'

'Because my phone ran out of battery.'

At that he just stared at her, his mouth ajar.

'I was distracted last night, okay?'

'No, it is *not*—'

'Is everything all right? I noticed the car broken down a mile or so ago…'

Zara jumped at the stranger's voice. She turned and saw that a man in a green four-wheel-drive had pulled up alongside them. She'd been too focused on Tomas—and too angry—to even notice the car thrumming behind her.

'Can I offer you a ride?' the man asked with polite concern.

'No,' Tomas answered in customary surly fashion, still glaring at Zara. 'Thank you,' he added shortly after she'd turned back and pointedly frowned at him.

'Tomas Gallo?' The man's face brightened. 'It is Tomas, isn't it? I've been hoping I might see you about.'

Only now did Tomas turn and actually look at the man.

'I'm sorry, I can't stop to talk,' he said curtly. 'I need to get Zara home—she's been out in the cold too long.'

'Oh, right. Of course. If you're sure I can't help…'

'Thank you but no. I can handle it from here.' Tomas reached for the bags Zara was carrying.

'Maybe I'll stop by the house some time…' The man trailed off when Tomas turned and looked at him again.

'Things are very busy for me at the moment,' Tomas said curtly.

It was a total brush-off.

'Er…okay, then.'

The man didn't offer them a ride again and Zara didn't blame him.

Zara didn't trust herself to speak until the car's lights had disappeared into the white. But as soon as they had she tightened her numb fingers around the plastic handles and pulled them away from Tomas's reach as she glared at him. 'I don't need you to "handle it from here".'

'No?'

'No. I don't need you to rescue me.' He'd done that once and it wasn't ever happening again. 'I am not incompetent.'

She was not the pathetic excuse for a human she'd once been. She'd studied. She'd got a job. She was making her own way. She was damn well happy for the first time in years. And she wasn't allowing him to make her feel inferior.

'No? You've been out walking in a snowstorm for hours wearing nothing but jeans and thin sneakers and a totally useless jacket. You're two minutes from hypothermia.'

'It hasn't been hours.'

'It's been three in total.'

Had it? Surely not. But she refused to try to look at her watch while he was staring so huffily at her. And frankly she was amazed he'd noticed what she was wearing or that he knew exactly how long she'd been gone for.

But come to think of it, she couldn't feel her feet or her fingers any more.

'Put this on.' He undid his coat.

'I am not wearing your jacket,' she spat.

'You'll wear it and like it.'

She tried to step around him to keep walking.

'Don't,' he warned her through gritted teeth. 'I am not in the mood.' He dropped the jacket around her shoulders.

'You're the one recuperating,' she argued.

'I'm ten times fitter than you are.'

That was probably true.

'And I am dressed for this weather,' he added pointedly. 'I have several layers on.'

Oh, he was just so perfect, wasn't he? In his leather boots and layers of wool and far too gorgeously broad shoulders.

'Give me the blasted groceries,' he bellowed when she resisted him taking them again. 'Stop trying to stop me from helping you. It isn't a crime.'

He confiscated the grocery bags, shouldered them and scowled at her. 'Are you sure you can keep walking? I have the car a little further back but decided to walk from there in case...' He trailed off, his frown returning.

'I'm *fine*.' She stomped her feet, hoping to thud some feeling back into them as she walked a step behind his punishing pace.

And she really was fine.

She was also furious.

Tomas could barely contain his anger. What the hell did she think she was doing walking out in this weather? How had her car broken down? As for her phone? Incompetent wasn't the word.

He'd been anxious about her for over an hour already. He'd had to phone Jasper to get her number and her phone had constantly switched straight to answer phone. That was when he'd really started to worry.

He hated worrying. He'd had to go out and find her.

And find her he had, smiling and basically singing to herself through a snowstorm. It was irresponsible and impossible and all he wanted to do was—

He stopped those thoughts in their tracks. They only made him all the more mad.

His anger continued to build as he got to his Jeep and threw her shopping onto the back seat. As he drove the final five minutes to home he noticed that she was suppressing her shivers. But his anger became incandescent when she shrugged off his jacket and determinedly set about putting the groceries away in the kitchen. As if all that were remotely important compared to her health?

'What do you think you're doing?' He glared at her.

'My job.'

He grabbed her hand to stop her, his grip tightening when he felt just how cold her fingers were. He swore beneath his breath then tugged her towards him. 'You're going to get changed, now.'

'What?'

He didn't bother answering, he just switched his grip

to her upper arm, wrapped his other arm around her waist and marched her from the kitchen.

'Tomas—'

'You're going to have a shower and get into some warm clothes,' he informed her as he half carried her up the stairs.

'This is ridic—'

'Your fingers are freezing. You should wear gloves.' He'd hunt some out for her tomorrow.

'I'm fine.'

'Maybe you will be. After you're warm and dry.' He walked her into her bedroom and released her.

But she didn't move, she just gazed up at him. 'Tomas…'

He couldn't bear to look into her radiant face—she was too pretty with those huge, expressive eyes and that sweetly curving mouth.

So he looked down at her wet jeans and refused to register the feminine shape of her legs. But he did notice and he didn't want to. He looked lower still. Her shoes were even wetter with their tangled, filthy laces. No way was she going to be able to undo those laces when her hands were that cold.

So he dropped to his knees and worked on the knots himself.

Zara stared, her heart arresting as Tomas knelt at her feet, intently working to undo her laces. She couldn't move. Couldn't think. He was so furious. So handsome. And so fantastically kind underneath all that gruff exterior. He finished undoing the laces and made her lift each leg to slide each shoe and sock off. Then he sat back on his heels and looked up at her.

Her heart turned over in her chest as she gazed into his beautifully dark and sombre eyes. She'd never known anyone like him. She'd never wanted anyone the way she wanted him either. And she couldn't hide it any more.

'Get in the bath or I'll put you in it myself,' he said softly.

That order melted the last frozen part within her.

'Really?' She couldn't help smiling at him. 'How d'you think you're going to do that?'

He looked up at her for just a moment longer—his focus dipping to her mouth. Then suddenly in one smooth movement he stood. Before she could step back he caught both her wrists in one of his hands and to her astonishment swiftly lifted his jumper and pressed her cold, cold fingers to his bare skin.

She gasped at the shock—and the sensation. She looked up into his face and saw how intently he was gazing at her. Her brain shorted out at the intensity in his eyes—and at the steady beat of his heart beneath her hand. His chest was rock solid and hot and her suddenly super-sensitive fingertips traced through the faint covering of hair.

'Tomas,' she whispered. Pleading. She couldn't help it.

He didn't reply. He just stepped that last inch closer and kissed her.

She moaned in instant delight, despite the fact his kiss was furious. He subjected her to the full force of his anger—and his passion—and both only brought forth the desire she'd tried to hold within herself for so long. But it was impossible to hold back under his onslaught. He overwhelmed every one of her senses. As she moaned again he pulled her closer, his hands roving down her spine to her waist and lower still, to pull her hips against his. She leaned against him, spreading her hands to explore more of his chest, loving the sensation of his hot, bare skin. She couldn't get close enough. He was so deliciously hard and she just wanted more. She could feel her toes now, curling them into the plush carpet as he kissed life and heat back into her.

The kiss deepened and, inexperienced as she was, she strained to get closer, knowing she had to get closer still. But he teased—his tongue wickedly curling around hers, then stroking within her mouth. So intimate and so in control. And so totally destroying her inhibitions. He broke away to press tiny, teasing kisses across her jaw and then down her neck. She arched, letting him caress that vulnerable, sensitive skin with his lips—and then with a gentle nip of his teeth. She gasped, shivering at the contrary sensation and he returned his attention to her hungry mouth. Her blood hummed as he ignited the most basic and undeniable of needs within her so easily. So desperately.

Closer. She ached to get closer.

She rubbed her fingers harder against his rigid torso, aching to feel more. She spread her hands that little bit wider, and rubbed the tips of her fingers against his tight, flat nipples. His arms tightened about her and his kiss became nothing short of ruthless. She bent back in his embrace, letting him plunder—wanting him to take more. Taste more. Wanting him to claim every part of her exactly like this. Completely.

She moaned again, her legs weakening, but he abruptly broke the kiss. He pulled back to look into her face and she couldn't stop smiling up at him, almost blind with sheer sensual joy.

Never had a man made her feel like this. Made her want like this.

He stared down at her silently, his breathing quick, his expression burning. But he didn't smile back at her.

Her smile faltered as she felt his tension growing—and it wasn't in a good way. Coldness stole back into her body as the tide turned. He straightened and so did she.

'Go and get into the bath,' he breathed, releasing her completely. 'Go. *Now.*'

'Y-yes,' she stammered. Then turned and fled.

CHAPTER FIVE

It won't happen again.

ZARA WASN'T AT all cold any more but she scrubbed her body all over—shocked and frustrated and *aching*. It was more than her body—her heart hurt too. Which was stupid because she knew he didn't feel the same way at all. He hadn't kissed her because he'd been thinking about nothing else for the last twenty-four hours. His action had been fuelled by anger, not lust. He'd only exploded because she'd defied him and he wasn't used to it. He'd been exerting his will…it wasn't that he felt *want* for her. It was just pent-up aggression.

But her feelings for him? Pure desire. She wanted so very much more.

And he knew it. Which was horrendously embarrassing.

Finally she made herself get out of the shower and dress. She refused to hide in her bedroom all evening, or, worse, leave. She wasn't running away from a difficult situation. She was staying to finish what she'd said she'd do. She'd promised and she was stronger now.

And that was thanks to Tomas. Not that he knew it.

He was in the kitchen when she went down to prepare dinner. He too had changed from his damp clothes, into a crisp black shirt and pressed trousers and loafers. He might have been aiming for businesslike but he just looked ruthlessly sexy to her. She glanced at the table to avoid staring at him like some lovestruck teen. The bags containing the groceries had gone. He must have put them away.

'I would like to apologise about what happened before,'

he said with grim deliberation, watching her from where he stood leaning back against the bench.

She flushed from head to foot but cleared her throat, determined not to sound as weak as she felt. 'I was as much at fault.'

After all, she'd encouraged him. She'd moaned. She'd clung and touched and—

'It won't happen again,' he continued as if she'd not spoken.

She nodded, annoyed as she felt her blush deepening. Because she *wanted* it to happen again. But he didn't want anything more. He couldn't look as if he wanted her less— his expression was so chilling. No doubt her over-the-top, sex-starved reaction had embarrassed him and he was trying to extricate himself from her neediness as quickly and firmly as possible.

Mortified, she couldn't bear to look him in the eyes any longer. 'I'll get on with dinner now.'

He nodded and walked out of the room.

She breathed out, both relieved and sorry at his departure. The only way she was going to get through the next day or two was to keep herself as busy as possible. But as she prepared the steak she'd bought in the village and chopped herbs and vegetables, her mind raced. She should tell him the truth about their past. That she knew so much more than what she'd admitted to him.

But he'd be angry and she didn't want to face that conflict alone—she wasn't as brave as she kidded herself. And she didn't want to hurt him. So she had to wait it out until Jasper arrived. But in the meantime she could get over her own weak desires and stay out of his way.

She already knew there was nothing worse than not being wanted.

Tomas walked back up the stairs to his den, distractedly gazing at the pictures in the gallery as he passed them. All faces he knew but didn't know. Faces he couldn't remember but that he'd since learned.

She'd smelt like sunshine after her shower. So contrary to the silent wintry storm settling in outside. He'd wanted her to come nearer instead of staying as far away as possible with the table between them. But what had happened *couldn't* happen again—even if she'd looked as if she'd wanted it to.

So he'd had to apologise and redraw the boundaries with her. He'd had to put distance between them again.

He had no idea how long it had been since he'd last had sex—and he certainly hadn't enjoyed any sexual relations over the last twelve months. Apparently he'd dated, but according to his research he'd never had any long-term relationships. That resonated as truth within him. Relationships—and family—weren't things he believed in. He had not had them, he would not have them. He knew too well that the only person he could rely on was himself. His own 'family' had taught him that well.

But he'd definitely forgotten how good it felt to hold a soft, willing woman in his arms. He stifled a groan; he was rock hard at the mere recollection of it.

He wanted sex. With her. Now.

He wanted it so badly he could barely think.

But he didn't want anything more than sex—no relationship, no opening up and emoting. No sharing of anything other than body and touch. Not with her or any woman. But he couldn't demand Zara's physical surrender and offer her nothing else. She didn't come across as a woman ready and willing for nothing more than a quick fling. Her eyes held too many secrets and sorrows. And with the painful truth about his mother, he could never have sex with a woman on his payroll.

But that didn't stop him wanting her.

He stared at the screens, forcing his concentration, slaving over the reports until he was up to date. He then opened up a new file. Then another. He sent screeds of emails to his staff working at the office in London under Jasper's eye—instructing him and them on what he wanted him and them to do. There was always more to do. More work to win. More opportunities to generate.

He just had to keep working. That was what he could control. And what he did best.

But then he heard the approach of soft footsteps and his concentration blew.

She didn't look at him; she was too busy watching that she didn't spill whatever it was she had on the wooden tray. He should stand to help and take it from her, but he found he couldn't move. Her cheeks were lightly flushed and her skin glowed and he couldn't look away from how beautiful she was with her hair half falling out of its ponytail and a smear of sauce on her white T-shirt.

'Here you go.' She set the tray down on his table. 'I won't be offended if you don't like it.'

She wouldn't even meet his eyes. Annoyance surged inside him again. He hated that apologetic tone from her. He wanted her smile back, together with that imp of defiance and the strength he knew she had when pushed. He liked it when she was true and not hiding.

'I promise I'll be honest in my assessment,' he muttered dryly, hoping to provoke a bite.

She glanced at him—a quick, sharp look—but said nothing.

Disappointment drilled deeper as he watched her leave the room. She'd basically run away from him and he didn't blame her.

He never should have touched her. He never should have let her stay.

He never should have hauled her close and kissed her like a dying man given his last, most desired wish.

He looked at the tray she'd put on the end of his desk. He wasn't hungry in the least but he didn't want to make her feel even more uncomfortable.

At the first taste he closed his eyes. The soup was full of rich flavour and hearty. The steak was tender and juicy. And the potatoes? It was comfort food and there was no mistaking it. God, it was delicious.

His mouth watered. For the first time in months he was ravenous.

It seemed she'd wakened two appetites within him. He could sate only one. But with each mouthful—as she filled one need in him, the other began to bite harder.

He wanted to carry the tray down to the kitchen and dine with her. Food this good ought to be shared—eaten at a table framed by laughing, talking people. But he couldn't. There was too much tension between them, too much need in him. And bitterly he suspected she knew more about him than he'd told her.

She knew something wasn't right.

So he savoured the dishes she'd prepared and brought his unruly body to heel with the determination that had made him recover so much of his physical strength. But he couldn't beat his own weakness. Not truly.

Sighing, he put the knife and fork down, unable to finish the last of it. But he had to be honest with her—at least in this.

She sat at the table, with her back to him, reading recipe books again. Her feet were bare and her slim-fit jeans and T-shirt emphasised her delectable body. It didn't need emphasising.

He tensed as his body swiftly reacted to her—that other hunger building to epic proportions. He gritted his teeth in annoyance at his base reaction. Being out of control like this was foreign to him, but at the same time all he wanted to do was indulge.

'Where should I leave the tray?' he asked roughly as he stopped in the doorway. He didn't trust himself to step a foot closer.

Startled, she turned, her eyes meeting his for the first time since they'd kissed. For a moment that passion hung between them.

She didn't speak. She didn't have to. Her eyes said it all. Shadowed and uncertain but with that flicker of desire that he knew he could bring to an inferno with little more than a kiss. What if he did more than that? How would she react then?

'It was delicious,' he said stiffly, determined to control himself. 'Thank you.'

'No problem,' she answered quietly. She stood and took the tray from him and then swiftly walked around to the other side of the table. Putting distance—a literal barrier— between them.

He leaned against the doorjamb, folding his arms across his chest, and glanced about the scrupulously clean kitchen. 'Did you eat already?'

She placed the dishes by the sink. 'I wasn't that hungry.'

He frowned. 'You should—'

'I ate as I cooked.' She turned and forestalled his lecture with a defiant tilt of her chin. 'The soup.'

At that he nodded, but he couldn't bring himself to leave her just yet. 'That man who offered us a lift earlier,' he said roughly, hating that he had to ask, but knowing he needed to for his own peace of mind. 'Had you met him before?'

She shook her head, her gaze now not leaving his. 'Had you?'

For the tiniest moment he felt like telling her. She looked so earnestly at him, her eyes soulful and her voice soft. But he didn't want to admit the truth and see her expression change. All he wanted in this moment was to forget it all.

The irony of *that* made him smile bitterly.

'You're a very good cook,' he muttered instead. 'That was the best meal I've eaten in a long time.'

'I'm glad you enjoyed it.'

It couldn't be more stilted. Allowing himself one last second to look at her, he straightened and headed back to his office.

Zara didn't feel the pleasure she'd expected from his concession she was good at her job. She wanted something else from him now and she couldn't get it.

She cleaned up the kitchen. Filling the late hours in the evening by scrubbing an already clean bench and floor and then wading through the next few books in the amazing cookbook collection she'd found on the shelf in the large pantry.

He didn't come down to the kitchen again and she didn't go to the office. She already knew he wouldn't want a hot chocolate or anything before he went to bed. She didn't bother with one for herself. She was still too hot.

When she finally made herself go to bed she found she couldn't sleep. She flicked the light back on and opened up yet another of the cookbooks. But her attention kept wandering—to those faint noises she could hear within the house.

Then the silence.

He would be asleep now. But still she couldn't find rest. Her brain had that kiss on replay. Her skin burned as the memory tormented her. Her muscles twitched as frustrated energy fired along her nerves. It had escalated so quickly. Total, raw lust.

She was so hot and flustered she couldn't bear to stay in bed a second longer. She sprang out of it and pulled on her jeans and a fresh T-shirt, not bothering to stop for underwear. In the dark she stole down the stairs to the kitchen because there was only one thing she could do. She'd work it out—physically and mentally and distract herself completely. She pulled out ingredients, piling them on one end of the table. She'd start with bread—make something that needed beating down over and over again. Just like this intense, unwanted lust he'd roused in her.

And she didn't care if he didn't like sugar, she did. She'd make biscuits. And cake. And pastry. And pies. Anything and everything to occupy her mind, body and soul until the sun came up and this impossible passion waned.

She flicked on both ovens. She'd try those recipes she'd been reading. She'd be so busy following instructions she wouldn't have the brain space to think about other things.

She measured. She chopped. She melted, smeared and mixed. She heated, stirred, glazed and—

'What are you doing?'

Almost dying of fright.

'Sorry.' He held up his hands as her scream's echo reverberated between them. He actually smiled. 'You do realise it's two in the morning.'

Really? She glanced at the clock on the wall and saw he was right.

Of course he was right.

She wiped her forehead with the back of her sticky dough-covered hand. 'Sorry if I woke you.'

'You didn't. I couldn't sleep.'

He too was in jeans and a T-shirt and no shoes, and with that stubble on his jaw and that burning look in his eyes all that effort in distracting herself was a total waste. She tipped the dough onto the bench and determinedly pressed it out. 'Why couldn't you sleep?' she said, just to fill the silence.

'My brain won't shut down.'

Her heart pounded harder and she squashed the dough into the wood. 'Work?'

'No.'

She met his gaze briefly, catching just a glimpse of scalding agony in his eyes. She looked back down at the mess she was making of the biscuit dough and knew she couldn't stay silent any longer.

'Would it help if I said I was sorry?' The words scratched.

'I don't want you to feel sorry for me.'

She looked up and met his eyes again but found she couldn't hold his gaze. It was impossible to be as honest as she ought to be. 'I don't—'

'I know you know,' he interrupted her harshly. 'I might not be able to remember many things, but I'm not an idiot.'

She put both hands on the table for balance. His memory. Amnesia.

He watched her relentlessly.

'Can you remember anything from before the accident?' she asked.

'I've lost about a decade.' His hands had curled to fists at his sides as he stood soldier-like on the other side of the table from her. 'Almost the entire time since I came to England from Italy.'

And how could she not feel sorry for him?

She cleared her throat. 'Do they think you'll get it back?'

'It's been a year since the accident. The longer it goes on, it seems the less likely full recovery is. But in truth, they just don't really know.'

'And you can't remember anything from that time?' she queried, her chest aching now. 'What about your work?'

'I read every damn textbook again.'

In the last year? She frowned. 'That's amazing.'

He shook his head. 'I have a natural aptitude for numbers, patterns. I haven't lost that.'

'But you remember everything—'

'Since I woke from the medically induced coma I was in, yes.'

She gave up on the biscuit dough altogether and moved to the sink to wash her hands. 'Your gallery upstairs...'

'Everyone I've met or had dealings with in the last ten years. Jasper has helped.'

'So no one knows?'

'Only my medical team. Jasper. My staff here. And now you.'

And no one else had the chance to find out because he'd locked himself away in this remote estate and refused to socialise with anyone.

She dried her hands on the small towel and turned to face him. 'Do you trust me not to say anything?'

'Do I have any choice?'

'I won't tell anyone.'

'Why won't you?' he asked. But his soft tone seemed dangerous. 'Why won't you sell your story?'

'Because... I just wouldn't do that.'

'Why not?'

Because she liked him and she felt loyal to him. Because he was her husband and he'd helped her more than he could ever know.

'Because that's just the way I am,' she said lamely.

'You don't want to hurt anyone.' An odd look crossed his face.

'I'm not a saint.' She grimaced. She didn't deserve his admiration at all.

'No?' There was a note in his voice that made her look up. A gleam warmed his dark eyes. 'You're telling me you've been naughty?'

That made her blush. His brows lifted higher but then the amused light left his eyes leaving them shadowed, the secrets hidden once more.

A harsh regular beeping interrupted. She turned, grateful for the respite. She grabbed the oven mitts and retrieved the tray from the oven.

'How hungry do you think we're going to get?' he asked dryly as she placed the chocolate brownie on the cooling rack. The bread rolls were already cool. As were the individual savoury tartlets. She figured the lemon shortbread mix might have to be ditched.

'Why couldn't you sleep?'

She could ignore that question, but she couldn't ignore what he'd admitted. She turned off the oven and then looked at him. 'It must have been very isolating for you.'

He walked to her side of the kitchen.

'Is all this pity?' He waved a hand at all her baking but she knew he meant her sleeplessness, her curiosity, her concern. 'Because that's not what I want from you.'

She couldn't move. 'What do you want from me?'

He was silent as he regarded her. 'Nothing,' he said almost inaudibly. 'I want nothing.' But he reached out and tucked a wisp of her hair back behind her ear. 'Except the truth.' His focus sharpened. 'Why did you come here?'

Yeah, he wasn't an idiot, he knew there was more to her story. Of course there was. But she couldn't bring herself to tell him. She didn't want to burst this bubble of intimacy and peace. 'Because Jasper asked me to.'

And that *was* the truth.

'Because you owe him?' Tomas persisted.

She nodded.

'He helped you once?'

She nodded again, her throat thick with unshed tears.

'He helped me too, once.'

'But you helped him. You got him out of that car...' She knew they'd crashed. That Jasper had been trapped and Tomas had got him free in an insane show of strength and determination. And yes, she was utterly in his thrall.

'Anyone would have done that,' he argued.

Not anyone. And not just anyone would have offered to

marry someone the day they met them to help them escape from an oppressive environment.

'Did he tell you about me?' he asked.

Her heart ached as she shook her head. 'He didn't mention it at all. Tomas…' She trailed off. The expression in his eyes was warm now and even though she didn't really believe in what she thought she was seeing, she didn't want to drive it away.

'What?' he prompted.

She couldn't tell him the truth, not now. But she couldn't ask him what she really wanted to either. She was still a coward.

'What do you want from me?' he repeated her earlier question.

It didn't matter. It wasn't right. And she was used to disappointment. But he moved that inch closer, his expression intense, his gaze focused.

'Zara.' He brushed the backs of his fingers along her jaw. 'Your skin is so soft.'

His focus shifted to her lips. She could almost feel the warmth emanating from him as he gazed at her. And she willed him to do what she was certain he was thinking about.

His lashes lifted and he looked directly into her eyes. Time hung suspended in the scented, steamed room. 'You're too much temptation.'

Before she could reply he brushed her lips with his. Too gently. Too briefly.

She drew in a small gasp of pleasure. Of disappointment.

But then he was back. She moaned as he claimed her mouth properly. He growled in recognition of her desire. He leaned her back, overpowering her completely until she caught his shoulders and all but collapsed against him.

Yes. This. *Contact.*

This was what she wanted. Him wanting her. Touching

her. Making her feel vibrantly alive. And in that instant she'd give him anything, as long as he kept touching her like this. He had one arm tight around her waist to support her, one hand holding her face to his. And his kiss? Pure passion.

He devoured her, there was no other word for it. And she was equally frantic—desperately meeting him slide for slide, lick for lick.

'You smell delicious,' he finally breathed as he broke from her lips to kiss across her jaw.

'It's the vanilla and sugar...'

'Not entirely.'

She smiled. 'You don't like sweet.'

'I was wrong about that,' he muttered, then returning to kiss her full on the lips again even as he straightened her so she could stand.

She whimpered as she felt him pulling back. She didn't think she could ever get enough of his kisses. But he smiled at her and grasped the hem of her top.

She froze but she didn't try to stop him when he tugged her T-shirt up and then over her head. In fact she helped, getting her arms free of the shirt. But she lowered her face, feeling the burn in her cheeks as he stood suddenly still and silent as he stared at her bare breasts.

Self-conscious, she glanced down. Her nipples were tight and tilting up towards him, inviting his touch. His tongue.

She shivered.

Her thoughts were so shameless they shocked her. But before she could turn to hide he grasped her waist with both hands.

'Zara...' He swept his hands up to cup her breasts. 'You're beautiful.'

She masked her inward grimace. She wasn't anything special but it was nice of him to say it.

'You are,' he insisted, gently swiping his thumbs across those taut nipples, making her quiver. 'I'll make you believe it.'

But he didn't kiss her again. Instead he stepped back and quickly yanked off his own shirt. She looked at him, her self-conscious awkwardness obliterated by sensory overload. Desire pulsed heat between her legs.

Now *here* was beautiful.

'Your muscles.' She gaped. They were so defined. So tight. She reached out without thinking, to trace another scar she'd not seen from the distance of her bedroom window when he was outside. His skin was warm and she stepped closer so she could feel more, pressing her palm flat against him. She wanted to feel *all* of him.

He clasped her close and kissed her again. Electrifying sensations ran untrammelled through her as his bare torso slammed against hers. She heard him mutter something but she clutched him that bit tighter because she didn't want him to pull away again.

He didn't. Instead he kissed her again but at the same time pushed her, backing her until her thighs hit the large kitchen table, and then he lifted her to sit on it. The pressure he applied wasn't harsh, but it was firm. Without breaking the kiss, he had her on her back and was leaning over her, his leg between hers—right where that ache was, where she needed him to press. She moaned as she felt his weight on her for the first time and she couldn't hold back from arching to grind herself closer against him.

A deep unbearable yearning opened within her. Instinctively she wanted more than all his weight; she wanted him to *pin* her. To hold her there, safe—yet so exposed—in his embrace. Everything was contrary. She wanted the same but more, slow but fast. She moaned, unable to voice her needs, and his mouth returned to hers. His tongue delved, filling one of the voids within her. She reached around him to run the tips of her fingers across his broad, strong back. He was so hot, his muscle so solid, she just craved *more*.

Her eyes drifted shut and she felt each of his touches more acutely. He threaded his fingers through her hair, holding her face to his, while with his other hand he caressed her breasts, shaping them, teasing them. Making her feel admired, treasured. Beautiful. He traced his fingertips, his palm over her body and all the while he didn't stop kissing her mouth as if it were all he'd ever wanted to do in life. Every moment of kissing sent her further along a path from which she wanted no return. She wanted to go further, never to stop.

His hand was now firmly down the front of her jeans, curving deep into her most intimate area at the apex of her thighs. Her eyes flashed open and she clamped her legs tightly together—half wanting to trap him, half wanting to stop him. She'd never been as intimate with a man before and she was suddenly embarrassed.

He lifted his head and met her tormented gaze. He didn't say anything. He just smiled with pure sensual intent. It was her complete undoing.

This was what she wanted. Him, warm and close and touching her and loving it. That need so deep within her spiked. His hand moved ever so slightly as he felt her heated reaction. His fingers stoked.

Her mouth parted but she couldn't form a coherent thought let alone actual words. His fingers stroked that bit faster.

He kissed her again. She had no resistance to his kiss. All she wanted was more.

Her embarrassment faded with every tiny, deliberate touch. All she wanted was to race along this path that seemed so imperative now. Urgency drove her own caresses. Tracing his broad shoulders and feeling the strong muscles rippling beneath his hot skin, she arched for more, rocking her hips against his clever, clever fingers that were still rubbing in that fantastic way. Tension built within her as he kissed her towards oblivion.

'Come for me,' he growled. 'I want to feel you.'

She writhed, embarrassment long forgotten in the heat of the passion he stirred within her.

'Tomas,' she begged, suddenly realising it was right upon her. 'Oh, no.'

She'd wanted to please him too—but it was too late.

'Oh, yes,' he muttered, lifting his head to watch her as he flicked his fingers relentlessly.

She ground hard against his tormenting touch, unable to control the writhing of her body, the shaking of her muscles, the moans tearing from her throat.

'Enjoy it.'

She shivered, instinctively twisting with unbearable delight. She screamed as pleasure pulsed, drowning her in tumbling, powerful waves. It was too intense. Too much. She shuddered, clutching at his shoulder to keep him close, to anchor her.

'Like that. Yes.' He kept her close, his satisfaction at her reaction evident.

Breathing hard, she gazed into his eyes for an age—he was so close, but still so unfathomable. She licked her lips, finally drawing an easier breath only to realise she was still hot. Still hungry.

That was when he kissed her anew.

She relished the invasion of his tongue. Desire flowed—renewed, strengthened. She curled her tongue around his, and then pushed past so she could explore his mouth. She wanted to give him what he'd given her. She wanted to see his satisfaction.

He let her play for a moment before asserting his dominance again, deepening his possession of her. He pressed harder against her as she lay spread before him. She couldn't help rocking against him as orgasmic aftershocks rippled through her.

'You want more,' he said bluntly.

Without bothering to wait for an answer, he unsnapped the fastening of her jeans and lifted her so he could slide them down her legs. 'No panties?' He flashed a sudden smile. 'Why, Zara—'

Stark reality hit, making her quickly sit up, drawing her feet up to the table and her knees high in a defensive pose. She'd never before been naked in front of a man.

He cupped her face, tilting it so he could see right into her eyes.

'The only thing I'm going to do,' he promised gruffly, 'is make you feel good. That's all I want.'

Her breathing quickened and she fought down her suddenly emotional response. No one had wanted to see to her needs, wanted to take the time to treasure *her* feelings. Not in years.

She wanted to say something, but her throat was too tight. Her eyes burning.

He kissed her. Light and gentle and questioning. She moaned, leaning forward to deepen it. So quickly and easily he led her into that firestorm of desire.

He put his hands on her knees and gently pressed them apart.

'Don't hide from me,' he muttered against her mouth. 'And don't hold back.'

She couldn't if she tried. Not when he kissed her like that. She let him pull her to the very edge of the table and then he stepped close again, right between her legs, so her most intimate part was pushed hard against his pelvis.

He was still in his jeans and she growled with frustration. She wanted to feel him this hard against her, but bared.

But he distracted her, kissing her breasts. Cupping them. Ever so gently kneading the full flesh, then nuzzling her puckered nipples, drawing one, then the other into his mouth to tease them.

She stared dazedly down at his dark head, watching his ministrations, the way he was almost worshipping her body, treating her with lavish care and attention. He moved lower, licking his way down her stomach, pressing her so she lay back down on the table. She gasped as he moved lower still, until he was right there, licking where she was most private. Most hot. Most wet.

She couldn't breathe. Couldn't move. 'Tomas...'

She didn't know if she was asking him to stop, or keep going.

His hands were firm on her thighs, keeping them spread so he could explore her the way he wanted to. The way she now wanted him to. Because what he was doing felt so unspeakably good.

His hand lifted, teasing her further apart, rubbing right where she was most sensitive. And then he was there, kissing her intimately, his tongue darted and circled, then he sucked her most sensitive spot. She gasped at how personal it was, how good.

He didn't stop despite her obvious surprise. And she didn't want him to. Not now. She rocked instinctively, her movements increasing the more he caressed her, until he was kissing her sex the way he'd kissed her mouth. Claiming full possession—deep and lush and unrelenting and she thrashed beneath him, desperately aching for the release he was pushing her towards.

'Please,' she begged, unable to hold anything back. 'Please, please.'

She thrust her hands into his hair, holding his head to her. But it wasn't necessary—he wasn't going anywhere. And he wasn't showing any mercy. He kept kissing, rubbing, sucking. He reached up with his hand to torment her tight nipple. She arched, her body locking on the brink.

She was going to die. She was almost in tears. She groaned again and again, her breathing ragged and desperate as she held fast on the edge as he licked her hot and fast. But she wanted more. So much more. She wanted him to feel as good as she did right now. She wanted *all* of him. In her. Coming with her. Feeling everything with her.

'Tomas,' she implored him rawly. 'Please take me.'

But he drew her nub into his mouth again and pulled, tossing her into that delicious abyss alone to scream loud and harsh as ecstasy overwhelmed her.

She didn't know how long it was until she opened her eyes again, but when she did it was to find him leaning over her and watching her close, one arm either side of her bared body. She couldn't move if she tried. But as he gazed down at her she slowly became aware of how she must look. A wanton woman, pleasured to within an inch of her life, spreadeagled before him. Not even in a bed, but on his kitchen table—as if she were the late-night dessert for him to feast on. And he had.

But now that sombre expression was back in his eyes.

'You should get to bed,' he said as he straightened away from her.

Oh, no, he couldn't do that to her *again*. His expression remote, he took her hands in his and tugged her into a sitting position.

He stepped back, almost angry.

Her courage crumbled. 'I'm not wearing anything,' she mumbled.

She wanted to get her clothes. Wanted to cover up and hide and run away to privacy to process what on earth had just happened. Most of all how he seemed to have rebuilt those barriers so horribly quickly. Unless they'd not really come down at all?

'Leave them.'

It was a harshly given order.

She was about to argue, determined to, but he didn't give her a chance. He gripped her hand in his and marched, not bothering to turn off the lights as he left the kitchen.

He held her hand as she walked alongside him up the stairs, unable to speak for fighting the disappointment crashing over her in waves. Those moments in the kitchen had been the best of her life. These were now not far from the worst. She was naked—utterly naked. And he was not.

She shivered as cold set in, covering her skin in goose-bumps. Inwardly she tried to process what had happened, but all she could think was that *he* wasn't satisfied. It was over and it had been so unfair. And she was so selfish all she wanted was more.

But he didn't. She could feel him pulling away with every step they climbed.

That disappointment morphed into anger. What had that been about? Had he wanted to secure her silence by se-ducing her?

Her heart turned to cinders as mortification burned her inside out. She was both hot and cold and so horribly un-comfortable, all she wanted to do was get away so she could hide how wounded she felt.

But he stopped by her door. For a moment he stood stock-still, not looking at her, as if he was picking his words with care.

'I shouldn't have—' He broke off as he turned and fi-nally met her gaze.

He huffed out a breath. 'Don't look at me like that,' he muttered angrily, his hand tightening on hers.

'Like what?'

'Like—' He broke off again, his expression tense.

'Like what? Like I'm confused? Like I feel used?' She squared her shoulders, damning the embarrassment to hell. She was naked and he'd tasted every inch of her body and made her more sensually aroused than she'd ever been in her life. And all of a sudden she was so cross with him because he hadn't let her do the same for him. 'Like I'm furious with you?'

CHAPTER SIX

'Please.'

'YOU FEEL USED?' he snapped.

She didn't get the chance to stalk off and slam the door in his face. Because he slammed into her—his kiss an explosion of passion and rage and need. He walked her backwards so quickly she stumbled and in the end he simply picked her up and dumped her in the centre of her huge bed. He instantly followed, his weight gloriously heavy and pressing her deep into the mattress.

'I want to make you feel good too,' she snapped her explanation when she finally got the chance to speak. 'I want you to—'

Her words were crushed again in his kiss. She held him to her as she had on the kitchen table. But she was over those jeans. As sexy as he'd looked wearing nothing but them, she knew he'd look better utterly naked.

'Let me...' she whispered, her mouth tender when he finally lifted his head long enough for her to speak again. 'I want to touch you. Turn you on. Make you—'

She broke off, finally realising the bluntness of her words. Words she'd never have dreamt of snapping to anyone ever. But they'd spilled out in her anger.

'You think I don't want you?' He shifted off her to lie on his side facing her. His anger was as apparent in the rigidity of his muscles. 'Touch me and find out for yourself.'

For a split second she just stared at him. But then she reached out.

She didn't really know what she was doing. She simply traced her fingers over his muscled chest and then she tracked lower, intently focused on what she wanted so much she shook with need. She struggled to undo the zipper, desperate to have him as naked as she was. Impatience made her fingers clumsy.

She heard his half-laugh and he moved, leaving the bed to stand and kick off his jeans. Her breath caught in her throat as she registered the magnificence of his physique. And the extent of that scar.

She scooted to the end of the mattress and reached out to touch him again before she thought better of it. Before he'd had the chance to get back on the bed. Before nerves made her shy. But instinct was riding her hard now—all she could do was touch him. Kiss him. Take him as deep as possible into her—wherever, however she could.

His breath hissed between his gritted teeth as she firmly palmed down his chest and curled her fingers around his rigid length. She glanced up at him, knew he was about to speak, but she held him fast and licked his tip just before he could.

His mouth parted, but no words came out. He stood, utterly rigid, his hot eyes staring at her.

She smiled—had she actually silenced him for a moment? Good. She kept her gaze on him as she lowered her head. Then she licked him again. She felt him jerk in her hand, so she tightened her grip then released to stroke upwards.

His breath hissed out again. She closed her eyes, and bent forward to totally take him into her mouth.

'Zara…'

She was still a little unsure of what she was doing, but quickly discovered that trying to give him pleasure like this only increased her own arousal. She panted as she rocked her hips in time to her rhythmic sucking. Oh, hell, she was so hot, and she couldn't get close enough again. Couldn't touch him enough.

She heard him swearing in a guttural tone. Then he stiffened under her hands.

'Zara,' he whispered. 'I... You...'

His hips jerked uncontrollably. She liked it and sucked him harder, deeper. That was the only answer she gave him.

He released a harsh sigh and combed his fingers through her hair, holding her head in place as he gave over to the urge biting him. She felt him trying not to thrust too hard but she wanted him to let go of his restraint altogether. Operating on blind instinct, she leaned closer and worked her hand that bit faster, rapidly tonguing his tip as she sucked as hard as she could.

His fingers were tight on her scalp as he tried not to push too deep into her. But she didn't care. She was too pleased.

When he released her with a shuddering sigh, she drew back to look up at him and smile. Now she felt better. Now they were almost even. But he didn't smile at her. His expression was fierce. He shoved her shoulders so she fell backwards onto the mattress.

'Spread your legs for me, Zara,' he ordered harshly. 'I need to taste you again.'

This time she didn't hesitate. Nor did he. He was there— kissing, sucking and rubbing right where she was wet and hot and almost hurting with hunger.

Relief swamped her for only a second before his sensuality sent her soaring. She wanted everything with him this time. Just this once.

'Please, please, please.' She couldn't contain her moans. She gripped the bedclothes beneath her as she arched up, offering herself to him completely. But he didn't let her have her release.

Not this time.

'I need to get something...' he growled as he pulled away with sharp, leashed movements. 'Just a second.'

That was when the reality hit her. He was going to give her *exactly* what she wanted.

'There can't be any consequences,' he said as he emerged from her bathroom carrying an unopened box of condoms.

Not physical ones. But she already knew there'd be implications for her. And she didn't care.

The dying firelight flickered, emphasising the angles and planes of his sculpted body with the warm glow. Her mouth smiled at the pure athleticism of him as he gritted his teeth and concentrated on the task of protecting them both. She wasn't surprised by his preparedness—there was everything a guest could ever need in that bathroom. She was pleased. Aroused. And slightly terrified.

He glanced up and caught her watching heavy eyed, her lips parted in admiration and anticipation. A muscle flinched in his jaw.

Maybe it was just that he'd been alone so long and she was here. That was okay. She'd take it. She wanted to give him pleasure, and relief, even for just a little while.

'Don't look so worried,' he muttered. 'I might not remember many things, but I don't think I've forgotten how this goes.' He knelt on the bed and leaned over her.

It wasn't as if she had the experience to help him. She should tell him. She knew she should tell him. But instinctively she knew that if she did, he'd stop and that was the last thing she wanted. He probably wouldn't even notice. If she just went with it. He'd made everything else happen so easily. So beautifully.

She wanted this. She wanted this more than she'd ever wanted anything. With a fierceness she'd not known she had within her she wrapped her arms around him and hugged him close.

He kissed her again. It was more familiar now, yet she'd never get used to how intensely and quickly his kisses could rouse the total wanton within her.

'You make it impossible for me,' he growled as he braced over her and nudged her legs apart with his knee. 'I cannot resist.'

'Then don't try,' she whispered. 'Please.'

She didn't care that she was begging. She just wanted him right there with her. In her. Fighting to reach that peak with her. And finding it.

She would give him anything. But she couldn't hold back the small cry as he pierced her physical purity.

He growled harshly and froze, his expression shocked.

She breathed out quickly, shifting beneath him just that little bit to ease the intense pressure she felt between her legs.

'Zara.'

She licked her lips and swallowed.

'I thought you said you'd been married,' he demanded her answer.

'I was…' She closed her eyes for a moment before making herself look at him. Making herself speak the truth. 'But he…he didn't want me that way.'

'He *what*?' Tomas stared at her, aghast. 'Did he have rocks in his head?'

She smiled ruefully. She could never answer that, not now. It was circumstances that were different.

But she saw the moment Tomas truly understood the implications of her words—of what her body had already told him.

'We should stop. This should stop.' He gazed at her with tormented eyes, but he didn't move. He didn't withdraw from her body.

'I don't want to stop,' she whispered. 'Please.'

He drew in a shuddering breath and she felt how much strain he was under to keep himself in check.

'Can't we just have tonight?' She wanted this one memory to treasure. She already knew no other man would ever make her feel this way. Never *want* in this way.

There might be regrets in the morning. But she'd never truly regret this. She wanted him more than she'd ever wanted anything. And she didn't care about the cost.

'You're a virgin.' He was still shocked.

Not any more. Not when he was there, inside her right now. And it was feeling so much better already. 'It feels *good*.' And it did.

He shook his head. 'I've hurt you.' But he was the one who looked pained. 'I didn't want to hurt you.'

'No.' She arched clumsily, trying to draw him closer still and tease those highly sensitive nerve endings again. 'The only thing that hurts is the thought of stopping.'

He was shaking with the effort of holding still. Beneath her back his hands had curled into fists.

'Unless you don't really want…' She trailed off.

Oh, heavens, that was it. He'd not wanted her before, why would now be any different? He'd been happy to fool around a bit but he hadn't really wanted her all that much.

'Zara.' His lips twisted as he smiled at her. 'Don't be an idiot.'

She tried to laugh but her heart squeezed.

'You know this won't be anything more,' he said. 'Just tonight. Just now.'

'Yes.' That was all it could ever be.

He kissed her. It was such a tender kiss that she thought he was apologising. That he was going to stop.

She held her breath as he braced on his arms and shifted, ever so gently pulling back. But then he probed deeper.

She moaned softly as a ripple of pleasure was sent from her core to every cell within her body.

'I'll make it better,' he muttered. It was a vow.

She fell a little deeper in love with him in that instant. He might have tried to distance himself from the world but he couldn't help but be kind when it counted. And he always put his own needs behind those of another. That was how he'd got so badly injured in the first place.

'It can't get any better,' she answered softly.

She felt him draw a sharp breath before he bore down on her again, watching her intently as he possessed her to his hilt. 'Yes, it can. And it will.'

She was like putty in his hands when he kissed her. She'd let him do anything and everything he wanted, as long as he kept kissing her like that.

Somehow she felt herself growing closer to him with every thrust. With every movement, every caress, he drew her further under his spell. She felt both protected and pro-voked—into opening up more to him, giving more. Taking more.

She grew greedy, raking her hands down his back to clutch and hold him closer to her. She arched, crying out in delight as he took her to the brink again.

'Please,' she begged, knowing she was so very close.

'You first,' he insisted, his teeth gritted.

'No,' she moaned. She wanted him *with* her.

'Yes.' He looked almost scarily determined as he bore down on her.

She trembled, her orgasm racking through her body. She'd never felt as exposed to anyone. Never so close. And never so good.

But as she sighed out the last of her release, she caught a pained look crossing his face and he thrust deep into her and held fast.

She cupped his jaw, forcing him to meet her eyes. 'Have I hurt you?'

A wry smile curved his mouth, despite the strain he was obviously under. 'It's my damn leg. I just need to…' He sighed, then held her super close and rolled, taking her with him, switching their position so he was beneath her and she sprawled over the top. All the while they'd stayed connected. And now that connection seemed stronger still.

More than physical.

Zara lay still for a moment resting on him, processing the shift—in both position and vulnerability. Ruefully he swept back her hair from her face.

'Sorry,' he muttered.

'No.' The sensation was something different again. 'Oh-h-h...' she breathed as she bent her legs and pushed her hands on his chest to lever herself into a sitting position. 'Is this better for you?'

He looked up at her and cupped her breasts, his small smile returned. 'I think I can live with it. Can you?'

Like this, he could reach down and stroke her just where they were joined. Just where she was so incredibly sensitive.

'Oh,' she moaned as he gently caressed her. 'I think so.'

He held her hips and slowly rocked her, showing her how to move on him. She bit down on her lip, testing pace, and then depth, watching his reaction as she did so. His eyes were almost black, and so focused on her. She felt so close to him and when she smiled at him, he smiled back.

She trailed her hand down his thigh, letting her fingers skim the scar. 'Better?' she asked softly.

He nodded. She was touched he'd not hidden that pain from her. And that he, like she, had not wanted to stop.

Sweat glistened, and his muscles rippled as he moved to complement her lead.

Being together like this felt so good. She leaned forward, pressing her hands on his shoulders as she settled into a rhythm.

'You keep making me come and you haven't,' she groaned, her head falling back as she began to crest the wave. 'Oh, Tomas.' She rocked harder, her instinct suddenly urging her to ride him fast. She threw her head back as her orgasm hit and she screamed her need for him. *'Come.'*

'Yes.' Hoarsely he gave in to her demand, thrusting up hard to meet her. 'Oh, hell, *yes.*'

This time she was the one leaning over and watching him. She smiled as he opened his eyes and looked at her. She was unable to think of a thing to say. There was nothing to say. She could only *be*—her body fizzing with warmth and satiation. But she smiled at him.

'You're still not tired, are you?' he teased, but there was a note of amused wonder in his voice.

'No.' If she'd thought her body was wired before, she was absolutely humming now. How could she ever sleep when she'd just experienced *that*? There was so much to process—she still couldn't believe it was possible to feel so good. For one person to make another feel this amazing. 'I don't think I'll ever be able to sleep again.'

He ran his hand up and down her thigh as he studied her. 'Then perhaps we'd better do something to fill in the time till morning.'

She shivered at the sensual promise in his low murmur.

'You're not sore?' he asked as he shifted under her.

'Not enough to care,' she said recklessly. 'You?'

'It's worth any amount of pain.'

She beamed at him. 'Then kiss me,' she asked shyly as she leaned down to him.

'Here?' He avoided her mouth to kiss her neck. 'Or here?' He scooted lower to catch the tip of her breast.

'Everywhere.'

She lost all track of time as he proceeded to do exactly as she'd asked. Lost track of the number of times she begged him. Lost track of where she started and he began. Lost track of almost everything but how good she felt.

And then she lost the ability to move altogether. She was so relaxed she was limp. She couldn't even roll to her side to face him.

'Sleep now,' he said quietly.

He kissed her. The softest touch to her temple. His passion had faded.

Her heart ached with the knowledge that it was over.

She kept her eyes closed because she didn't want to see the finality in his expression. She just wanted to curl against him and pretend a little longer except she hadn't the energy to move closer.

But then she heard the door snick. She snapped her eyes open and realised she was alone.

CHAPTER SEVEN

'The good feeling doesn't last.'

THE KITCHEN LOOKED as if it had been struck by a tornado.

She was going to have to scrape the dried biscuit dough off the end of that table with a jackhammer. She couldn't bear to look at the other end where she'd lain like a sexual offering to the lord of the manor.

There was no sign of Tomas. Not for the entire time it took her to scrape and scrub the table clean and do all the dishes she'd left out from her midnight bakeathon.

But then the door leading to the garden opened.

'What would you like for breakfast?' she asked as he silently stalked in.

He looked wind-bitten and irritable and too many muscles were on show in those shorts and T-shirt and trainers.

'I've already eaten.' He didn't even look at her. He didn't need to. The glower on his face said it all.

He wanted to be beastly again? Fine.

'I'll prepare lunch and let you know when it is ready,' she replied *faux* sweetly. 'I won't bother you again before then.'

He hesitated at the door and then swung back to face her. 'What happened last night was a mistake. It won't happen again.'

'That's what you said about that kiss,' she pointed out. Did he really think it could just be forgotten about?

Maybe it could. And maybe he regretted it completely.

He didn't answer. Didn't apologise. Didn't stay another second.

For a moment she leaned against the bench, absorbing the stab in her heart. Then she pulled herself together. She wasn't going to pine for his attention. Instead she point-lessly rubbed the silverware she'd found in the room to the left of the kitchen. It was so highly polished already she was making no difference, but she needed to do something.

Her anxiety was building, threatening to tear her apart.

She should tell him the truth. She *had* to tell him the truth. Especially now. But she couldn't bring herself to do it. Not without Jasper there to confirm it.

Tomas glared at the date and the name he'd written on the blank page in front of him, forcing himself to resist the almost overpowering urge to race back downstairs and apologise and pull her into his arms and do everything all over again. He couldn't believe his idiocy. How could basic instinct and lust dominate his reason so quickly or so completely?

It was because of the proximity, right? The weather out-side made everything inside seem more intimate. He'd been there and she'd been there and they'd been alone and she'd been willing. So very willing.

He frowned.

Why had she let him do that—why had she said yes to him so quickly, when she'd let no other man before? He hadn't earned the gift of her virginity. She barely *knew* him.

It didn't make sense.

His suspicions sharpened, arrowing in a direction he re-ally didn't like. She knew about his memory loss and then she'd let him do anything he wanted to.

Jasper's words lingered with him—that recommenda-tion to have some fun and 'come back to life'...but Zara wasn't one of Jasper's 'good time girls'. She was as sweet as she looked. And vulnerable.

Jasper had told him that too. He ripped the page from his journal and screwed it into a ball and tossed it into the fire.

He'd made a hash of everything. He didn't want to lead

her on. Didn't want her thinking there could be anything more. Because there couldn't be.

He was furious with himself. How could he have been that out of control? Was he that starved of sex? He'd barely thought about it these last few months. He'd been too busy working on his physical health, on his business, on reclaiming control of his life. Yet at the first opportunity he'd got—with the first woman who'd crossed his path in months—he'd pounced. He'd stripped her on the kitchen table and ravished her, barely giving her a chance to catch breath before beginning again. She'd come here as a temporary employee and he'd taken advantage of her in every way possible.

It had been horrendous behaviour.

And what would she be expecting from him now?

He didn't have anything to offer her or any woman. He'd kept his distance deliberately to protect his reputation, his business. The truth about his injury could never become public knowledge. But it seemed he needed to protect a woman from himself too—from his new rabid, uncontrollable lustiness.

He'd failed Zara as her employer. He wouldn't make that mistake again. He'd take control of his sex drive and leave her alone. It was only a few days and she'd be gone.

He ignored the raging tension in his body at the thought of denial. He wasn't letting lust overrule him—not when he'd overcome so much else.

He clamped his teeth together to stop himself from speaking to her when she brought up a tray with his lunch. His jaw ached with the effort.

A shadow entered her beautiful blue-green eyes as she placed the tray before him.

He ignored it—her, the tray, his own desires. He had to. He had to re-establish distance—coolness—between them.

She got to the doorway before she turned.

'You know, I get that last night was a one-time-only thing and that you don't want any more than that,' she said softly, only the faintest shake to her voice. 'So you don't need to be this rude to me. I'm not hanging around for more. You're not going to break my heart or anything. But you could still be polite.'

He stared at her, stunned at her annoyance. Annoyed at himself because she was right. He had treated her exactly as he'd once vowed never to treat any woman. He'd acted as if he'd *used* her. No woman deserved that. 'I apologise,' he said formally. 'I didn't intend to be rude.'

He glared after her as she stalked away, her back ramrod straight and her chin held high.

He had been a jerk. He wouldn't blame her if she didn't want anything more from him—except he didn't think that was quite true. Those sea-green eyes couldn't hide much—certainly not the way they deepened in colour when she looked at him.

He sighed. He'd been horrible. She had been a virgin, and he hadn't even bothered to stay and cuddle her to sleep after he'd finally been spent.

He was appalled with himself. Most of all because he still wanted more. He just didn't understand how he'd lost control of his desires in this way.

Zara pressed a hand to her chest as she ran lightly down the stairs, her legs wobbly from literally standing up to him. When really, she had nothing to stand on when she'd been the one keeping information from him.

But it was meaningless information really. What was one day? It hadn't meant anything to him. Nor had last night. And that was okay.

She bent over her work again. A long while later she heard him stomping down the stairs. She concentrated extra hard on the piece she was polishing.

'What are you doing?' he growled at her.

'My job, what do you think?'

'You barely got any sleep last night—'

'So? That's not stopping you from working.'

'That's different.'

Oh, that got her riled. 'How so?'

'Mine isn't physical work,' he said gruffly.

'This isn't exactly that hard.'

'But—'

'Don't try to stop me. What happened last night hasn't changed anything,' she argued. 'It's just a job. I'm being paid to do this job. If I don't do the job then what am I being paid for?'

He paused. An almost stricken look entered his eyes.

'Exactly.' She smiled sharply up at him in victory. 'I'm doing the cooking and the cleaning, Tomas, and you're not stopping me.'

'Fine.' A muscle jumped in his jaw. 'Just don't overdo it.'

'I pride myself on doing the best I can, just as you do.' She shook her head. 'Please don't patronise me.'

He huffed out a frustrated breath. 'Please don't be so damn prickly.'

Her jaw dropped. 'Look who's talking,' she bit back sharply.

He stared at her for a second. And then his smile flashed. Reluctantly at first and then it became broad and wide.

He shook his head. 'You don't make this easy.'

'You don't think?'

Too late she realised the implication of her words. Hadn't she been totally easy?

He threw her a stunned look and burst into laughter at her mortification. 'You're blushing.'

'Don't comment on it, you make it worse.' She glanced at him, then started to get mad at him all over again. 'Don't do that.'

'Do what?' He grinned.

Look gorgeous. Look human and hot and fun. She turned it on him. 'Are you really going to spend all day ignoring me and then decide to be nice just because you're bored again?'

'I'm not bored,' he answered ruefully. 'I could never be bored with you in the house.' His brows pleated. 'Last night didn't happen because I was bored.'

Flattery wasn't going to work. She refused to let it.

'You're not bored either,' he added thoughtfully. 'Are you?'

'How can I be, when I don't know if you're going to bite my head off or try to—' She paused in her retort.

'Or what?' He dared to grin at her.

'Do something…unspeakable,' she finished.

Something gleamed in his eyes but he straightened and pressed his knuckles against the table. 'Why did you do it?'

She paused. Knowing what he meant but not wanting to answer. How could she explain it to him?

'You were a virgin.' He crossed his arms and glared at her.

'Does it matter all that much?' she asked, more bravado now than honest. Because, yes, to her it did matter. But she didn't regret it. She'd *never* regret it. And she wasn't going to let him taint the memory of how perfect those moments in his arms had been.

'You met me less than forty-eight hours ago.'

She swallowed. How could she tell him now that she'd fantasised about him for a *year*?

'And you let me do all that and more. More than once.' He shook his head. 'Why?'

She didn't know how to answer him.

'Did Jasper send you here to seduce me?' he asked. 'Did he pay you to…entertain me?'

'Are you honestly asking me that? *Again?*' Angrily she

tore back at him. 'You think I'd really do that?' She rose from the table and stomped towards the door. Unfortunately that meant she had to stomp past him. 'No money would be enough for me to do that. I can't and won't ever be bought.'

He grabbed her as she made to get past.

'Then it's because you feel sorry for me. Because of my injury.'

His hands were firm on her waist and it took every ounce of willpower to suppress her trembling. But to her surprise he was pale—as if he really questioned why she'd slept with him.

'You think I held onto my virginity all this time only to give it up out of pity?' She shook her head because he was crazy. 'If I felt sorry for you I might make you a cup of tea and cook you your favourite dinner…but I wouldn't let you *inside* me.' She was so emotional she couldn't hide her shaking now. 'I wouldn't ever be that *intimate* with a man just because…'

His eyes narrowed as he ruthlessly watched her. Making her admit it all.

'So if it wasn't because of those reasons, then why?'

But saying it was so much harder than showing him. 'It's much simpler than that. I let you have me, because I wanted you. I wanted you so much I ached. I couldn't stop and I didn't want to.'

'So it was just lust?' He looked disbelieving.

'Why did you sleep with me, then?' She turned the tables crossly. 'Why did you…do all that to me over and over and over when you'd only just met me too? Even when you realised how inexperienced I was…'

'No, I didn't want to stop. You're gorgeous.'

'So I can't lust after a guy for his looks, but it's okay for you to lust after a woman?'

'But I wasn't a virgin, Zara.'

'Like that matters all that much?'

'Doesn't it?' he dared her. 'You said it yourself, why would you have held onto it all this time? If it didn't matter all that much, why were you still a virgin at this age?'

How could she tell him she'd been unable to look at any other man in that way since she'd first met him?

'You're saying I'm old?'

He laughed and gave her a gentle shake. 'No and don't try to change the subject. I refuse to believe this was the first chance you'd had to have your wicked way with a man. If you'd wanted to, and if it didn't matter to you all that much, you would have lost your virginity years ago.'

Silenced, she looked at him.

'So why me?' he pressed her. 'Why now?'

She swallowed. 'You have a very beautiful body.' She faltered. 'And very beautiful eyes. You're…fascinating.' She was simply absorbed by him. 'And you're very good at kissing me,' she whispered.

'Kissing turns you on?'

She touched her tongue to her lip very quickly, but he saw. He saw and he knew.

'Has no one else ever kissed you?' he asked softly.

'Not the way you do.'

'How do I kiss you?'

She gazed up into his eyes and one secret thought spilled out. 'Like you can't get enough of me.' As if he were pouring every ounce of himself into her—and it made her so warm, so beyond herself.

'Well, that's true,' he answered almost inaudibly. 'I can't.' He cradled her face in his hands. 'You like to feel wanted? Is that what it is?' he asked. 'Because, sweetheart, you have no idea how much I want you. How many times I want you. But I can't do anything more than want you just for now. Do you understand?'

'What I understand is that in a couple of days I'll leave here and most likely will never come back. I'll get on with my business and you'll get on with yours,' she answered. 'I don't want anything more from you. I won't take anything from you. Other than...'

'Sex.'

She nodded, wincing a little at the blunt admittance.

'You'd better mean it, Zara. Because if you agree to this, then, I have to warn you, it's not going to be a restful couple of days.'

Her breathing quickened. She was aroused at what he was implying. 'You mean—'

'I mean if you say yes now, I'm likely to want you every damn moment from now until you walk out that door and drive away. But when you do drive away, you mustn't look back. You mustn't come back. Not ever. You promise me you can do that? You promise me you won't want more. Because I haven't any more to give.'

She didn't care how needy she was, how accepting of what little he had to give. Because the truth was she had no more either. This was all she wanted from him because it was all she could have. Once he knew the truth he'd be so mad with her, but she was too selfish—and too hungry— to deny herself just this little time.

Because what Tomas didn't know was that this would end the second Jasper arrived and the truth came out. There was only this night before the lawyer was due. Tomorrow it would all be over.

'You won't come back,' he pressed her.

'I won't.' But only because he truly wouldn't want her to.

He pulled her close to him. 'Promise me.'

'I promise.'

He kissed her, instantly sending her back into that cauldron of desire. She flung her arms around his neck and kissed him back. She was so mad with him. But as she rubbed against him she felt just how aroused he was. He walked her backwards until her back hit the wall.

Not the table this time? She tore her lips from his so she could look into his eyes and read his intent. To see if he was as wild as she.

In answer he reached into his pocket.

'You have a condom with you?' She glared at him accusingly. 'When you were so *rude*?'

'I'm sorry,' he muttered, quickly kissing his way to her forgiveness. 'I'm very, very sorry.'

And suddenly she was even more turned on. And even more angry.

'Then maybe you'd better use it.' She fumbled, but somehow yanked his trousers open.

For a second he glared back at her. Then he fought to get the condom on fast enough. As he worked she undid her jeans and shimmied them and her panties down. Finally sheathed, he pushed her so her back was right against the wall in support.

But then he hesitated. 'Zara—'

'Take me,' she said, daring him. Daring *herself.*

'You're not ready.' He shook his head. 'You can't be ready.'

'I've been ready all day,' she said scornfully.

His pupils dilated. Without breaking that searing eye contact, he slid a firm hand up her inner thigh, not hesitating to go higher, to stroke her and find she was right.

His word was short, pithy and to the point. And he'd stepped up before he'd finished saying it.

She screamed raw victory as he bucked hard and filled her right where she needed him. *Physical.* That was what this was. For the first time in her life she was in thrall to unrefined, hot lust. And it was the best thing ever.

Tomas watched the savage emotions flicker across her face as she first softened, then tightened about him. She couldn't hide it from him—the need, the rapture she felt as he took her. Saucy little moans spilled from her mouth as he thrust again. Hot desire flooded him, blinding him in a flash to everything but the need to feel her even more. *Now.* He thrust harder, his need overtaking him sooner than he'd ever intended.

'Zara,' he warned her hoarsely as he felt his control slip. But she was too slippery, too hot, too welcoming and his body's demands drove him on. He needed to get deeper inside her. Deeper, harder, faster. He grabbed her, lifting her a fraction so he could.

'Yes,' she cried as he uncontrollably rammed into her over and over. 'Yes. Yes. Yes.'

'Oh, Zara.' His world splintered as satisfaction gushed through him, out of him, and into her. Too soon. Too damn soon.

'Tomas!'

His relief was multiplied tenfold as he felt her come hard at the exact moment he locked into her in his one last, fierce thrust to orgasm. They clenched together for a long moment. Both shaking, revelling in the wild pulses of pleasure.

Then he pressed his head against her shoulder, breathing hard in recovery. He half laughed. That had been too fast to count.

But for the first time in months he felt wholly strong again. He wanted to prove it, to revel in it and take every pleasure with her. Sex with Zara made him feel invincible. Not even his leg seemed to bother him as much today. Maybe this was the exact kind of workout it had needed.

He kissed her deeply, then led her back to her bedroom to reposition her on her bed, determined to take it slower this time. Wanting to show her every way he could think to pleasure her. Her eyes widened but she welcomed him with that hot, sweet enthusiasm of hers. He wanted to hear her scream his name again and again. He wanted to feel the dynamism in her body, and then feel her fall soft and relaxed and curl into him. Sated and sweet and sexy.

But her lids grew heavy again as she drank in his body when he pulled away after the second time, to fetch them both a drink of water.

Insatiable minx.

'So you didn't give me your virginity because you were in love with me?' he teased as he lifted the glass to her lips as she lay sprawled in a tangle of sexiness on the bed.

She spluttered as she sipped and took the glass from him with a baleful look.

'Were you in love with the woman you lost your virginity to?' she asked him with a frown. Then her eyes widened in horror. 'That's if you... Oh, I'm sorry.'

Her blush was beautiful.

'Actually, yes, I do remember it, because I wasn't as old as you when I lost it.' He half laughed at her concern.

His sexual awakening had been during the torment of his mid-teen years when he'd been on the streets and hustling cards to survive.

She was silent a second. 'Were you in love with her?'

He shook his head. He was never in love with anyone. And wouldn't be. He didn't really know what love was. But he sure as hell knew what it wasn't.

'I was tired and alone and she made me welcome.' He set the water down on the table beside the bed. 'She did things that made me feel good and showed me how to make her feel good too.'

She'd shown him that sex didn't have to be anything other than a physical pleasure between two willing partners. That was all it had to be. Nothing tacky or a sleazy transaction, but nothing meaningful either. Just release. And for him, that was all it would ever be. Except he'd forgotten just how good it could feel.

But hedonism took you only so far.

'But?' she prompted, sensing his hesitation.

'The good feeling doesn't last,' he admitted, needing to warn her. 'Other things get in the way.'

'What other things?' She looked wary.

'Other wants.'

'She wanted what you couldn't give?'

'I wanted different things from her,' he clarified. 'Don't be mistaken, there was no love between us. No heartbreak. We were together only a handful of times before it ended.'

But he remembered too well the fine line it was between mutual pleasure and the need for more. What people would do when they were desperate. He'd vowed not to take advantage of the vulnerable in the way that people had tried to take advantage of him as a youth. Of the way people had taken advantage of his mother. And he knew how vulnerability led to temptation. Selling out might seem like an easier option, but it had only led his mother to destitution and despair.

He'd fought a different battle, leaving Italy to further his prospects in England—knowing he needed education and opportunity. He'd worked to gain both. He'd worked hard.

Zara had quietened as she watched him remembering.

He frowned, knowing if he thought too much further there'd be too much he couldn't remember. The darkness would settle.

He moved so he could tease her most sensitive parts as gently as he could.

'How is it possible it can feel even better than before?' she muttered dreamily as she arched into his embrace.

His arms tightened about her. She had a point there.

CHAPTER EIGHT

'Would it be so awful if the world knew?'

'THE SNOW IS too severe for Jasper to drive,' Tomas announced as he walked into the kitchen in the late morning.

The knife clattered on the bench as Zara quickly put the bowl she was holding down. She licked her lips, pretending to focus intently on the cake she'd been icing. 'So he's not getting here today?'

Her heart had been racing all morning—her whole system in a state of high anxiety, knowing the axe was about to fall. Knowing she should have said something sooner.

'He thinks tomorrow or the day after should be fine.'

Another day. She breathed out. She had been granted one more day. She still couldn't bring herself to say it. Not when she could have a few more hours of bliss.

'Can you do something for me?' she asked, her voice catching.

He angled his head. 'Depends what it is.'

Yeah, there was no automatic reply of 'anything'—he was still wary. And she didn't blame him.

'Try these and tell me which you prefer.'

He looked at the two slices she'd plated up and pushed towards him. 'They look the same.'

'Can you just try?'

'You know you don't have to go to all this trouble just for me.' He smiled wolfishly. 'Though I do appreciate it.'

'It's not for your benefit.' She rolled her eyes, muttering caustically, 'I'm testing recipes.'

'Oh, now I see.' He smiled as he bit into the first piece. 'So I'm just your guinea pig.'

'Lab rat, yes.' She smiled, relaxing as she teased him.
It was fun teasing him.

'Recipes, huh?' He pulled her notebook around so he could read it. 'May I?'

'You already have.' She pushed a piece of the second slice towards him.

His brows lifted as he flicked through the pages. 'You have a lot of notes.' He glanced up and levelled her with a piercing gaze. 'Does the world really need another baking blog?'

'Does the world really need another rich recluse?' she countered pleasantly.

He laughed. 'Touché.'

Impatient, she watched as he bit into the second piece. 'So which do you prefer?'

He took his time, watching her as he savoured the slice. 'They're both delicious,' he pronounced, picking up her recipe book to rifle through it in greater depth.

'That's not helpful. I actually need a decision.'

'Can't do it.' He glanced over the page and shrugged at her. 'They're both so good.' He put the book to the side and picked up another small piece of cake. 'What else have you got?'

'A lot, as it happens.' She stepped to the pantry and came back with the container of samples she'd been working on.

'What are you going to do with all of them? If not a baking blog.' He watched as she selected a couple of biscuits and added them to his plate.

She smiled but shook her head. She wasn't about to tell him. Not when he made his fortune predicting the success or otherwise of companies. Especially when he did that with incredible accuracy. She didn't need to be shot down quite so soon.

'I won't steal your idea.'

She laughed at the thought of Tomas up to his elbows in

flour and white icing. 'I don't want to give away the recipes, I want to sell the product myself.'

'Go into manufacturing?'

'On an artisan scale, not mass produced.'

'For farmers' markets and the like?'

Of course he'd grasp it right away. She nodded. 'I've been selling some of my products at my local one for a while and a couple of the nearby cafés have asked me to supply them.'

'You're a baker more than a housekeeper, then?'

'Yes, but I need to work while I get established.'

'Of course.' He picked up another biscuit but studied it rather than eating it. 'You've had training?'

'I learned a lot from my uncle's chef and I took a course this past year.'

'Full time?'

She nodded. 'I need to do more but at the same time—'

'You don't want to wait to get your business under way.'

'Yes.' She felt self-conscious about sharing her ambition with him. No one had ever believed in her, least of all her. 'I know it probably won't work—'

'Why wouldn't it?' he argued matter-of-factly. 'According to the newspapers I built up my business while studying.'

She put down her container and sent him a look. 'You're not like most people.'

'I'm not?'

'You work harder than any normal person can. You have more focus and drive than anyone I've ever met.'

'Maybe it comes down to motivation, then. How badly do you want to succeed?'

'You must want to succeed very badly.'

'When your life depends on it, I guess that gives you focus.'

Why had his life depended on it? Where was his family? She was so curious and he couldn't really help her. She wished she could help him. But the only thing it seemed she could really do was 'entertain' him.

Which, frankly, she loved.

'Speaking of work, I have to go do some now.' But for the first time in ages, Tomas didn't really want to. He wanted to stay near and talk to her.

'So when you said we'd be at it every moment, that was an empty promise?'

He nearly choked on the cake. Was that a sultry taunt from his blushing lover? 'I'll be back downstairs later and you will pay for that.'

'Will I?' She looked all innocence.

Now there was a challenge from her. Eyes narrowing, he walked closer to her, smiling as the colour ran up under her cheeks.

It took little to arouse her. A fact he relished given he permanently ached for her. For her touch.

So touch her he did. Until she was soft and hot and whispering those pleas in that broken voice. And then he stopped, leaned against the bench as he half growled. 'How badly do you want to work now?' he challenged her.

'That's mean,' she breathed balefully. 'That's so mean.'

'You do the same to me.'

She distracted him. Tormented him. Made him want to cast everything else aside and only be with her.

'Then go away so we can both concentrate, please,' she begged.

She was right. He needed to leave before this escalated further. As it was he'd been late starting because he'd gone back into her room to wake her.

He backed out of the kitchen, his gaze trained on her the whole time.

'Stop it,' she mouthed.

He was rock hard and aching but he forced himself to

leave the room. He was still in control of this situation and himself.

But less than an hour later he was pacing in his large office. This distraction had to stop. Thing was, he knew it was going to. She'd leave soon enough. His housekeeper would return. There was only today. He'd been disciplined for so long, what would one afternoon cost?

He went down to the kitchen but found it empty; only her music and the lingering scents of lemon and vanilla were there to remind him of her. His mouth watered. He paused in the hallway, listening for sounds. Then headed back up the stairs.

She'd not gone to the left wing—where he worked and their bedrooms were—but the right. She was in the drawing room, peeking under the drop cloths at the furniture that had been covered for storage. She'd opened up the shutters so the light was let in and she was really being nosy.

He leaned against the wall and watched her move around the room looking at each object in fascination.

'What are you doing?' he asked when he realised she still hadn't noticed him.

She whirled in surprise but then that dimple popped and her eyes were glowing.

'Snooping,' she confessed as she failed to bite back her smile. 'Do you have any idea how amazing this stuff is?'

He lifted away from the wall and walked towards her. 'I've seen it.'

'It seems such a shame to hide it all away.'

'There's no need for me to have every room ready. I can't be in all of them at once.' He knew the house was too big for him. But he'd wanted space.

'It's like a museum.' She walked across the room. 'You bought it furnished?'

He nodded. He hadn't bothered to look too closely at all

the treasures. He'd just turned a small part of the place into what he needed as quickly as possible.

'But you then covered everything up?'

'Are you judging?'

'No. I'm exploring. It's fun.'

She lifted a small clock from a nearby cabinet and brought it to him. 'This should not be hidden away.' She gave him a stern look. 'This should be enjoyed.'

'I don't know that it even works.'

'So what?' She held it to the light. 'Shouldn't we just enjoy the decoration of it? The beauty?' She placed it back on the cabinet. 'Small things,' she muttered. 'All the small things.'

He watched as she uncovered more treasures. He refused to feel guilty about them; some time they'd be on show again. But her appreciation of them all got under his skin. He couldn't help smiling at her animation. She was a conundrum: the way she handled the objects led him to think she'd been around valuable things before, but at the same time she showed an almost naive enjoyment of them.

'I suppose I'd better get back downstairs.' She suddenly sent him a guilty look.

'Yes or I'll start cracking the whip,' he said dryly.

She laughed even as that gorgeous blush swept under her skin. 'I was taking my duty as housekeeper very seriously and checking on the condition of the rooms.'

'Of course you were.' He walked with her down the corridor towards the stairs, thinking he'd sidestep with her into her bedroom. All he wanted to do was kiss her.

He noticed her looking at the pictures on the wall as they passed by. He grimaced. He knew it was weird, but it was a system that had worked for him.

She suddenly stumbled.

'Are you okay?' he asked.

When she straightened he noticed she'd paled.

'Are you hurt?'

'No.' She kept walking, her pace quicker.

He didn't believe her. Something had bothered her. He glanced back along the row of photos they'd passed.

'Which ones are your ex-girlfriends?' she suddenly said, switching on a bright smile. 'Don't they get their own corridor?'

He hesitated, still certain something had upset her. And it wasn't going to be any ex-girlfriend.

'I'm picking this one.' She pointed to a picture of a willowy blonde.

'She's the wife of one of my main clients and never, ever would I consider it,' he answered dryly.

'Because she's the wife of one of your clients?'

'No.' He rolled his eyes. 'Because she doesn't attract me in that way.'

The colour had returned to her cheeks and she took a step closer to him. 'You prefer brunettes?'

His lips twitched.

She sent him a swift look from under artfully lowered lashes. 'And shorter rather than tall? Perhaps with blue-green eyes?'

'You wouldn't be fishing for compliments, would you?'

'If I were, I'm not getting any bites.' She sighed mournfully.

'I can bite if you really want me to.' His voice dropped as his blood stirred. 'It's just a question of how hard.'

Quite the apprentice minx now, she was getting good at the art of distraction. And for now he'd go with it. He liked seeing her sensual confidence blossom. 'For the record, none of these women were long-term lovers. Apparently I worked more than played.'

'And that's still true.' She actually pouted.

'I think it's true for you too.' He walked with her past

more rooms in which the furniture was covered up and hidden from the light.

'You know, I didn't think you'd care so much what people think.'

'I don't.'

'Oh?' She turned away, innocently. 'Then why do you go to such lengths to hide from them?'

He shot her a look. 'Don't try to change things for me, Zara.'

'You're not just a bit lonely?'

'No.'

'Yet...' She trailed off.

He turned to glare at her. 'This fling we're having isn't because you're the first woman who's been to stay here with me.'

She smiled weakly.

'I'm not that much of an animal and you're more of a treasure than you believe.' He frowned. 'You need to value yourself more.'

Zara snapped her spine straight at his zinger but she ignored his point because she knew what he didn't. She knew the truth. Before his accident he'd met her. And he *hadn't* wanted her.

She wasn't a treasure—not then or now. What was happening between them now *was* because of circumstance. Because of his loneliness and a basic instinct that needed fulfilling. The fact that he'd denied it showed he'd thought about that himself.

And that was okay.

'If you're not hiding, then it wouldn't be a problem to have other people to stay,' she pointed out.

'It's not possible,' he said gruffly, that finality in his reply. 'And it's not what I want.'

Her heart thudded as she saw just a glimpse of emotion in his eyes. But she had to press just a little more. He was locked away in this beautiful home, not even enjoying all of it. It seemed such a waste to her—most especially of his life and what he had to offer.

'Would it be so awful if the world knew?' she asked.

He straightened his shoulders. 'My clients would lose faith in my investment choices.'

She shook her head. 'But your company has done better in this last year than any other previously. Wouldn't that cancel out any criticism?'

'Doubt would begin to creep in,' he replied, all authoritative businessman now. 'There is no room for any doubt. There must be unshakeable belief.'

'But people know you're human. You're not an oracle. Certainly not made of stone.' Though he looked it now.

'I never would have remained in place at my company if I hadn't been sure of my ability to do my job,' he said sternly. 'I've lost many memories, but some things are still there. Just as I know how to brush my teeth, I can still see the patterns and understand the numbers... But I employ a number of people and I need to be mindful of their position too. That is why Jasper is currently the public face of the company and he's doing a good job. Eventually I will return.'

'Will you? When?'

'When I am ready.'

'Really? You really see yourself breaking out of here and going back to London?'

'Don't you think I can?'

'I think you can do anything you set your mind to. It's whether you really *want* to that's the question.'

He gritted his teeth. 'I'm happy here.'

'You're *safe* here. That's a different thing.'

'Is it? Doesn't being safe make me happy?'

'Maybe there would be other things to be happy about.

And are you truly safe or are you constantly worried you're going to get found out?'

Wasn't that why he'd been so reluctant to even open the door to her? Wasn't that why he never went into the village? He was *trapped* here. And he shouldn't have to be.

He didn't answer.

She ventured closer. 'Have you forgotten anything else since the accident?'

'No,' he answered tightly. 'But that's not to say it might not happen. I work hard to keep my memories.'

'What do you do?'

'I write a daily journal. Archive articles and so on.'

'You hoard newspapers?' she teased gently.

'Online. Sure. I keep a record of every conversation. Every interaction. Every decision.'

'Do you have a record on me?'

'Yes.'

'Do I get to see it?'

'No.' He almost smiled then.

'How detailed is the record?' She suddenly couldn't meet his gaze as she realised the implication of what could be in his journal.

'Not that detailed.' She heard the smile in his voice. 'I've found it difficult to know what to write. Although...' he paused wickedly '...maybe I should detail it all. Looks to me like you'd be curious to read it.'

She shook her head.

'What can you remember before the accident?'

'You want to know what my childhood was like?' He walked ahead of her and then turned to block her path. 'You want to analyse me?'

'Is there something to analyse?' she countered, knowing she was too curious. But she wanted to help him somehow.

'Maybe. As much in me as there is in you.'

'I'm not afraid of telling you my story,' she said quietly.

'I had a happy childhood here in England until I was twelve and then my parents died and I went to live with my only living relative—an uncle in the Caribbean.'

An uncle whose photo was upstairs in his gallery. A small, single photo. A sparse single sentence detailing an invitation. No mention of his ex-wives. Or of her. She'd nearly fainted when she'd spotted it.

He looked startled.

'I know.' She shrugged ruefully and tried to make light of it. 'I don't look like I ever lived there. I have no tan. Never could get a tan.'

'It wasn't a happy time?'

She shook her head. 'I hadn't known him. Neither he nor his wife knew me before they flew in to rescue me. But I wasn't what they were expecting.' Or wanted. 'The first day with them in their home isn't something I can ever forget.'

'What did he do?'

'Owned a casino, not a very successful one.'

'No,' he said slowly. 'What did he do to *you*?'

She hesitated.

'He hit you?'

'Only a few times.' She'd learned what not to say and when to keep out of the way. But sometimes there had been no avoiding him at all.

'Once is one time too many.' Tomas frowned. 'Being hit hurts.'

She interlaced her fingers to stop herself reaching out to him, knowing that if she made a fuss he'd stop talking. 'Someone hit you?'

He met her gaze with a wry twist to his lips. 'Lots of someones. Lots of times.'

Goosebumps riddled her skin and she felt as if a chasm had opened up at her feet. One false move and she'd fall. She didn't want to fall, she wanted to understand. She wanted to care.

'Why?' she could only whisper.

That wryness faded as steeliness replaced it. 'My mother was a whore.'

She flinched but managed to hold in her gasp. He'd chosen that word to shock her; he was watching too closely for her reaction.

But her next reaction was unstoppable. A deep, painful pity rose—his poor mother. And poor Tomas. 'She must have faced some very tough times.' Zara picked her words carefully, but knew they were useless platitudes.

He hesitated a second, then it seemed the words spilled out, even though she sensed he didn't want them to.

'She became pregnant with me when she was fifteen. Her parents were not supportive. She ran away to the city and once there…ruin. Unfortunately I was left to grow up in a small village in rural Italy where such mistakes of morality were unforgivable.'

'She gave you up?' The poor woman had been little more than a child herself. 'You lived with your father?'

'Who knows who he was?' He dismissed the idea bitterly. 'A village boy, most likely. One who did not step up to his responsibilities when my mother's pregnancy was revealed. No, I was brought up by my mother's father.'

'Didn't he protect you?' Zara's heart lurched painfully. Or had he been the one to hurt Tomas—making the child pay the price for the mother's mistake? And what had happened to his mother? There was such deep hurt there. Years of hurt.

'He was the one who refused to allow my mother to stay. She came to him when I was four, desperate to return home. He allowed her to leave me, but not stay herself. He hit but only to discipline. It was the other kids who hit—cowards who attack only when they're certain of winning. In groups, against the smaller or weaker. Bullies.'

'So you were shunned.'

'Of course.'

Had there been no one to love him? And now he chose isolation. Because not even his family had offered the protection a child should have by right.

'Do you forgive her?'

He stared at the door, his face an expressionless mask. 'What is there to forgive her for? Desperate times force people into desperate acts. She did what she had to, to try to survive. The world's oldest profession.'

'No,' she said softly. 'For leaving you.'

Because even though she knew it was possible to understand on a rational level, it still hurt emotionally. She still hurt that her parents had died, she still hurt that her uncle hadn't cared for her at all.

'She made her choice,' he answered almost robotically. 'She had no choice.'

'Have you ever seen her again?'

His lack of reply told her it all. And now her eyes watered at the image of a small boy left alone to face the judgment of a closed community. And for a desperate mother who'd done what she'd thought was for the best.

'Don't cry for me, Zara. It is so long in the past. They can't hurt me any more.'

Couldn't they? Couldn't those memories hurt? Couldn't scars stop skin from stretching properly again?

'So what did you do?'

'I ran away,' he said simply. 'I was fifteen and I'd had enough.'

'Where did you go?'

'Milan initially. Then I travelled across Europe to London.'

'You weren't scared?'

'All the time.' He grimaced. 'The thing I remember most is the hunger. That fear of not knowing where your next meal is coming from. Of not knowing where I was going to sleep that night. I remember making the decision and feeling that drive to get me there.'

'You still feel that drive?'

'Like it was yesterday. So if you want to analyse, you could say it's the need for security that drives me.'

'Financial security?'

'What other kind is there?' He shook his head and smiled as if she were totally naive. It wasn't a nice smile. 'Love doesn't last when you're starving and have nowhere to sleep. It doesn't feed you or shelter you or even keep you warm. Not for long. You need money to survive.'

'And that's all you need? Just money?'

'Some would say money can buy you everything else you need,' he said. 'It can't for everyone. But it can buy all *I* need.'

She disagreed. She'd had shelter and warmth and food. But she'd had *no* love. And as a result, she'd had no life. Sure, she'd not been starved physically, but emotionally?

That hurt. In a different way for sure. But it still hurt. It still damaged.

She figured they both deserved more.

'A fortress with a big wall,' she said sardonically. Hiding away from the rest of the world wasn't what anyone needed. Not for ever. He was as human as she. And humans needed companionship. They needed love.

She needed love—to give it and be given it.

'Privacy. Space. Time.'

She almost laughed but it was too sad. 'You don't have any time. All you do is work.'

'Work will always be my focus, I'm not going to apologise for that.'

She didn't expect him to. She understood how important a fulfilling career could be. She just didn't believe that he was as hundred per cent happy as he claimed. And of course he wasn't with the injury he'd suffered.

'No balance, then, huh?'

'It's what I like. It's what gets me up in the morning. I like the challenge of it.'

'There are other things you like,' she argued. 'You shouldn't isolate yourself.'

'And you're the expert?'

'I am, actually. I was isolated when I went to live with my uncle. I let that happen. I didn't stay in touch with friends and people who could have helped me sooner. And I became so unhappy it was hard to help myself.' She admitted her weakness. 'I lost all my confidence. But now I'm getting it back and I won't lose it again.'

'Is that right?' His voice lowered.

A frisson of danger rippled down her spine as he faced her.

'What happened to make you lose that confidence? *Who* happened?' He walked closer. 'Was it your husband?'

'Sorry?' Zara asked, hoping she'd misheard him.

'There's no need to apologise,' he muttered as he intently watched her. 'Just tell me about your husband.'

Her scalp prickled. She supposed she'd asked for it, what with chiming in with her opinions on how he was living his life. But she really couldn't answer his question.

'Why did you marry him if he didn't want you in "that way"?' he prompted when she remained silent.

'It was a convenience thing,' she finally answered.

'Convenience?' Tomas looked mystified. 'Was he gay and had a disapproving family or something?'

Did he think that because her husband didn't want to have sex with her? She smiled wanly. 'No, it was more complicated than that.'

His eyebrows shot up. 'More complicated how?'

She should tell him, confess it all this second. But she couldn't. How did she tell him how weak she'd been?

'He helped me out of a situation…' she began but faltered. She tried to walk past him but he reached out and snagged her hand.

'You don't want to talk about it?' His thumb swept over the back of her hand. 'Yet you ask me personal questions.'

'I was curious. I'm sorry.'

'No apologies,' he reminded her with a low mutter. 'I want to know more about you. You're the most interesting woman I've met in a long time.'

'We both know I'm the *only* woman you've met in a long time.'

'And we both know *that's* irrelevant.' He drew her that little bit closer, but he didn't pull her all the way into his arms. 'Tell me.'

'There's not that much to tell.' She tugged her hand gently but he didn't release her. 'It was never intended to be anything more than a temporary thing.'

His eyes narrowed on her. 'But you cared for him.'

All the air left her lungs. He was too astute. And suddenly she was too scared.

'More than he cared for me.' She shook her head at Tomas's frown. 'That was okay. He was a nice person. He was honourable.'

'Was?' He looked concerned. 'He died?'

Almost.

She bit her lip. 'No, but he's no longer in my life.'

Not for real. These few days didn't count.

He let go of her hand. 'I'm sorry.'

'Why?'

'Because that saddens you.'

It did.

'I think I've left the oven on,' she invented, wildly flustered and too near to tears. 'I'd better check it.'

CHAPTER NINE

'She made her choices. Now you make yours.'

TOMAS LET HER RUN. It was obvious she was distressed and he didn't want to upset her more. He walked into his office and closed the door, determined to shut her out and himself in. A low ache throbbed in his temples. He needed his peace, solitude and space back. But tumbling thoughts hounded him. He should not have pried. Why did he feel this nagging need to know everything about her? Let her keep her secrets. Heaven knew he had his. But God only knew why he'd blurted half of them to her just then. Telling her about his mother? About the stupid bullying he'd suffered as a kid? Why had he done that?

He'd been a child. It was over. He was over it all.

Yet for some reason he'd wanted to see her reaction. He'd wanted to shock her, to see if it would drive her away.

But she'd crept that bit closer, her big eyes holding such tender concern and inviting confession. Looking at her, he'd lost control of his own emotion. The scalding hurt that nowadays seemed to lurk so close to the surface had broken free and he'd spilled too many of his little secrets.

What a fool.

But she had her hurts too and that angered him more. The shadows in her eyes had darkened with wariness when his questions had got too direct.

That shouldn't bother him, but it did. And the fact that he was bothered at all bothered him all the more. Because this fling with her meant *nothing*. It had to. He'd not got as far as he had, as quickly as he had, twice over, by getting distracted or invested in other people.

'She made her choices. Now you make yours.'

Nonno Gio had been blunt to the point of cruelty, informing him that his mother hadn't cared enough to want to keep him. That he was on his own. For years he'd not known that his mother had begged Gio to let her stay too. That it had been Gio who'd refused. Tomas had been led to believe she'd just dumped him and run.

'It'll be better here, Tomasso. You'll be happy here.'

He remembered her voice. Remembered her crushing embrace. He'd been so angry because she'd lied. He hadn't been happy. And so yes, for a long time he hadn't forgiven her.

Because from the age of four he'd been tested again and again, through isolation and intimidation, unsupported through the trials with his classmates, even his cousins. Nothing he'd achieved had been good enough—not even when he'd topped his class in every subject, every damn year.

Nothing he did could pass as penance for his mother's indiscretions. Gio just waited for him to slip up and if he ever did, he came down hard. And then, in the heat of another argument with the old bastard, Tomas had learned the truth. That his grandfather had forced his mother to choose between a certain home for Tomas without her, or a life with her on the streets. It had been no choice for her.

And no choice for him either. He'd run, hoping to find her. He never had.

He'd learned early on, more than once, that the only person he could truly rely on was himself.

Yet he'd not even been able to do that much in this last year. His amnesia had weakened him in a way he simply couldn't tolerate. The only way for him to fight it and move forward was to focus on his company. To make it secure. To *succeed.* On his own.

Hours passed by incredibly slowly as he reined in his

wayward concentration. A semblance of peace returned to him as he studied reports and checked on the market fluctuations. This was what he knew. This was what he did best.

But in the late afternoon he heard the music coming faintly from the kitchen. No doubt she was in there baking up a tsunami of sweetness. They were going to be buried in biscuits at the rate she was going. His stomach rumbled. Maybe a little sugar wasn't such a bad thing.

He glanced out of the window at the view across the garden to the wall and the snow-covered fields beyond. The church spire in the centre of the small village was only just visible through the lightening clouds. The locals would be pleased the bad weather was lifting, the farmers' market was on early in the weekend and attracted many people to town. Jasper would be able to arrive and she would leave with him. That was good.

But an idea occurred to him. One he couldn't resist. It would be easy to arrange and amusing to watch. He wanted to see her dimple peep when she smiled one last time. He picked up his phone and put his rusty voice into action.

Then he made himself work some more. He had to pay before their final moment of lightness and pleasure. But in the end the temptation grew too strong.

He silently prowled down to the kitchen. Sure enough, she was there, meeting his stare with pink skin tinged with sugar and eyes filled with cautious reserve.

He stopped just inside the door, forcing his muscles to stillness, but his body was a riot of want. He blatantly stared, trying to read her thoughts—her desire. Because he didn't want to ask, didn't want to talk. This couldn't be about talking or sharing. This could only be about the physical pleasure and release they found with each other.

'Come upstairs with me,' he asked. His voice sounded husky and alien to his own ears.

She didn't speak, but she moved. Slowly she walked

towards him. His muscles tightened with every step she took, at the acceptance and anticipation in her gaze. His desperation burned through his reserve. Finally she was near enough for him to touch. A feral growl escaped him. He didn't give a damn about the twinge in his leg as he lifted her up. He just had to hold her. Had to have her. And it had to be now.

Zara rose super early again the next morning. She'd been unable to sleep once he'd gone from her bed. And he'd left her only moments after tearing her soul apart with pleasure.

It had only been the once and that devastated her. Was he trying to pull away? Did he want this to be over? Had that conversation yesterday been too intense for him?

Intuition told her the truth.

This wasn't what he'd wanted. He lived here in isolation because he liked it that way and he wasn't planning on changing any time soon. That awareness made her heart ache.

'You're baking at stupid o'clock again?' His dry question interrupted her ruminating.

Startled, she looked up and forced a smile at him. 'It's not that stupid.' It was only a little after six in the morning now. 'There wasn't much other work to do. I didn't think you'd mind.'

'I don't mind.' He reached over the kitchen bench and snaffled one of the warm cupcakes. 'But I think you have far too much food here for us to eat. It's just going to waste.'

'That doesn't matter. I was only trialling some recipes.' She hadn't made complete batches, she'd been switching up different ingredient amounts and additions to test new flavour combinations for the fragrant shortbreads. So far she had lavender, violet, pineapple, sage and primrose.

'It's not good to waste food, Zara. There's a ton of hungry people out in the world,' he chided gently.

She smiled for real as she transferred biscuits one by one from the tray onto the cooling rack. His mood had lightened; that was good. 'What do you want to do with it?'

'I've booked a stall at the farmers' market today.'

'You've what?' She nearly dropped the tray and all the biscuits on it.

He grabbed the end of the tray, rescuing their load. 'Let's see how well they sell.' He grinned at her.

'Oh, no.' She put the tray carefully on a board and wiped her hands on her cloth. 'They're not good enough. I'm not ready. Don't they need to be inspected by the food police or something?'

'Stop panicking and relax. It's fine. I checked with the manager of the market. He's going to bring some supplies so you can bag and tag the goods before we start. Your baking is delicious and we're not throwing it in the compost. Give it all away as free samples if you like and ask people what they think of it. You can think of it as product-testing research.' He leaned against the table, a curious smile hovering at his mouth.

She breathed in and straightened up as she began to think about it properly. In all, it wasn't that bad an idea.

'I've put a fold-up table by my car already,' he added helpfully.

That was when other implications of his offer hit her.

'You're going to take me into the village?' she clarified.

He was going to leave his lair to help her out on this crazy whim?

'Sure, I'll drop you in there.' He straightened and turned away.

Did that mean he wasn't going to stay with her? Because she really wasn't sure she wanted to do this on her own. Not in a new village. At least up north she'd had one of her fellow students with her to keep her company when she'd started in the market round there. And she did want *him* to stay with her. She wanted him to get out and have some *fun* outside his cave. Even on a frosty cold morning.

'I thought you could go through the cupboards to choose some plates or something to display them on,' he said, distracting her completely. 'You need to be quick though—the market opens in ninety minutes and you need to get set up.'

She didn't even have any signs made up. Or prices. Or a cash float...

But maybe she could wing it. Giggling to herself, suddenly giddy with excitement, she spent twenty minutes poring over the fine china. There were so many beautiful treasures she was scared of breaking them. 'Are you absolutely sure about this?' she asked as she handed a box of her selections to him. 'Some of these are worth a lot—'

'They're just sitting in storage.' He shrugged. 'It's good for them to be used.

Tomas loaded the boxes and the table into his big four-wheel-drive.

'Stop looking so scared,' he teased. 'It'll be fine.'

It wasn't so much the market that she was scared of. It was him leaving her right away to go back into hermit-man mode.

The market was larger than she'd expected and quite the beautiful affair with charming displays and beautiful hand-crafted goods and foods.

'I'm not dressed well enough,' she despaired as she checked out the 'posh country' attired women.

'You look good enough to eat,' he murmured, a lewd look in his eye.

'But I don't have bunting. Or fairy lights. I can't compete.' She half laughed, but felt more like crying as nerves threatened to get the better of her.

'You have antique crockery, sweetheart.' Tomas waved one of the priceless plates at her before carefully placing her decadently iced violet cake on it. 'You don't need to compete.'

But once he'd helped her set up the small table and bag the bulk of biscuits and cake slices, she clutched the sleeve of his thick coat. 'Please don't leave me alone to do this.' She hoped it wasn't bad to call upon that chivalrous instinct she knew he had.

'Zara, I can't stay—'

'Of course you can. You don't have to give your name. No one will recognise you behind the sunglasses. And with the woollen hat you look like a tourist or something. Truly. Please,' she begged him. 'Please, please, please. Please stay with me.'

All of a sudden that plea had a whole other meaning to her, and too late she realised she'd sounded *too* heartfelt.

He gazed at her, an arrested expression in his eyes as he wavered. Then he blinked and expelled a sharp breath. 'Ten minutes to get you started, then you're on your own.'

She was so happy she beamed at him, swiftly reaching up and pressing a quick kiss to his lips before she'd thought better of it. 'Thank you.'

Ten minutes into it there was no way he could leave; there were too many people crowding the stall. Forty minutes into it they were in danger of running out of stock.

'I'll go get the rest from the car, you stay here,' Zara said while he was dealing with a customer, quickly leaving before he had time to turn and argue with her.

But she slowed as she carried the last two boxes back to the stall. He was in full flight, smiling and talking to the group of customers who were basically breathing in the biscuits and exclaiming about their delicacy. But they all had eyes on Tomas. It wasn't just his looks, it was that smile and that charming way he looked and talked to them, as if they held his undivided attention. And she knew holding his attention felt like the best thing in the world.

Clearly she wasn't alone in having that reaction to him. He had that rare ability to draw people near—old, young, female and male—they were all there now. He'd made her small stall the most popular at the market. It was that undeniable, undefinable X-factor.

'Zara is the baker.' He called her over as he spotted her hanging that short distance away. 'She's the one who made them.'

She had to walk forward then and unload the last supplies.

'I should go back to the car,' he said when a brief quiet moment finally happened.

'No, you have to stay. You're my customer magnet.'

'Your *what*?'

'You heard me.' She giggled, then sobered when she saw his look. 'It's not that any of these people have any idea who you are,' she assured him saucily, her success loosening her tongue and her inhibitions. 'And it's not that you're super-rich and successful because they don't know that. It's because you're big and tall and handsome and you have this sexy accent and a gorgeous smile and you look at people like...' She shrugged, unable to express it. 'You're a charmer.'

For a half-second he just stared at her. But then he laughed and, heaven help her, became more attractive than ever.

She shook her head in mock distress. 'The thing is, I'm not really joking. It's all truth.'

Tomas picked up the last piece of cake and munched on it to save himself answering her. But he didn't leave. He couldn't. Not when she was so radiant and smiling at him. Not when he was having this much fun.

They didn't make it to the end of the market—they'd sold

out too quickly. But they took the time to walk around and check out the other stalls. He loved watching her touch the soft wool scarves on display, and seeing her sample some of the rich cheese. He gave in to her demands and tasted some too, and had to concede that it was divine. *She* was the magnet—her vitality intoxicating.

He was almost sorry when it was time to leave. She helped him pack everything back into the car and jumped up into the passenger seat. Once he'd started along the narrow road back to his home she turned to him, her joy obvious and overflowing. 'That was just amazing.'

Tomas grinned as he listened to her non-stop recap of the morning's trading. She was aglow with her success.

'They loved the primrose snaps, did you notice that? They just disappeared so quickly. And *you*...' She turned that brilliant smile on him once more. He could almost feel the warmth hitting him. 'They just loved you.'

'No, they didn't.'

'Oh, yes, they did.' She nodded, a small frown pulling her brows. 'Especially that woman with the reddish hair. She kept coming over to sample stuff just so she could smile and talk to you some more. Like *all* the time.'

He couldn't help a small chuckle at that small truth. He wasn't sure if she'd have noticed that, given she'd been so busy herself. But despite the obvious play that woman had made for him, he'd enjoyed the market more than he'd ever imagined he would. It hadn't mattered who he was or what he'd forgotten. He'd just stood alongside Zara, laughing and talking to people about nothing in particular, feeling more free than he had in aeons.

'It was just so cool,' Zara said again. 'Thank you so much.'

He smiled, pleased she was happy and enjoying her endless chatter as he navigated his way home.

'It's such a beautiful house,' she enthused as he drove

down the snow-lined driveway and the manor came into view. 'Do you know what you should do? Open it up to weddings—and other functions. The kitchen is big enough to be upgraded to a full commercial size. I could serve cream teas. With that garden and the greenhouse, it's just such a gorgeous destination and so suits my kind of traditional baking with a twist. Don't you think?'

She was in raptures, and, while he still smiled at her enthusiasm, his core was growing colder by the second.

She had good business instincts and rationally he could see these were all good ideas that could work well. But the thought of her remaining here? Working here as chatelaine of his estate?

He tightened his grip on the steering wheel as all pleasure was decimated. His gut reaction to her plan wasn't favourable—but for all the wrong reasons. He didn't want her baking all hours in that kitchen for everyone else. If she was baking in that kitchen, he wanted it to be for *him* and him alone, not the rest of the world. He didn't want to share either his house—or *her*—with anyone else. When she'd asked him to stay with her? He'd been unable to resist.

But the idea of her staying here with him long term?

It was impossible.

His heart raced as bitterness surged. He was no better than that fabled dog in the manger. He couldn't have her but didn't want anyone else to have her either. The realisation appalled him. He couldn't be *jealous*. He couldn't want more than these few days he'd already had with her. He couldn't have that. He'd *never* have that. He knew what was best—and for him, it was best to be alone. Utterly independent.

This morning had been a mistake. He'd known after their talk yesterday that it was time to pull away from her, but he'd failed. He had to do it properly now. Get back to work and distance himself from the warmth of her.

Having anything else with her—or any other kind of life—was an unsustainable fantasy. He might have got away with a couple of hours in public one morning without anyone figuring him out, but he couldn't risk more than that.

'I need to catch up on my work,' he said briskly as he parked the car. He walked straight to the door, unable to even look at her in his haste to get away. 'Do not bother with dinner for me tonight. I'll have something at my desk later.'

Zara bit her lip, fighting her blush. But he walked away without a second glance so what did it matter that she was probably as red and bruised as a crushed tomato?

He'd dismissed her. It was as if the sun had gone behind a monstrous storm cloud, leaving the once warm world cold and dark.

But she'd been the one to summon the cloud. She'd been so stupid, totally overstepping the mark blurting all that fantasy. What had she been thinking? Of course he wouldn't want all that. He didn't want *her*—not for anything more than a short-lived fling.

It had been obvious enough yesterday that he was uncomfortable with how much he'd told her. He'd clammed up and in a way she'd been glad because she hadn't wanted him to keep asking *her* questions. She hadn't wanted to admit the truth to him yet.

But the real truth was that she didn't belong here and she never would.

His coldness had shattered the happiness she'd felt from the morning at the market. He was so very controlled, locking his emotions tightly back behind that fierce guard. And wasn't that fair enough? Didn't he have enough on his plate already without her being emotionally needy and placing demands on him that he had no desire to meet?

She needed to grow up. To protect herself the same way he did. To lock her heart away in that layer of protection.

So she wouldn't let him see her insecurity now. She could get through this last day without awkwardness. She'd stay in control and keep it light. And then maybe, when the truth did come out, when Jasper explained everything, maybe everything could *stay* okay. Maybe they could even become friends once it was all revealed.

Her heart squeezed, knowing the futility of that hope.

But she had to get through this. She'd lift her chin and let him know he wasn't going to hurt her—because she understood that was a big part of his motivation for pulling away. He'd never wanted to hurt her. She didn't want to hurt him either. So she could handle this and respect the boundaries he needed.

'I know you only wanted a small snack, but I've made it for you anyway.' She placed the small tray on the edge of his desk in the early evening, almost six hours since she'd seen him last.

'Thank you.' His smile was small and set and he looked straight back to the papers in front of him.

Despite her best efforts, she was still too soft. Disappointment slithered down her spine as she walked away from him. She'd made a mistake in taking her talk too far, in encroaching on him. But she had to make this end easier for them both. She had to be like him. She had to be brave.

CHAPTER TEN

'You're a bad influence.'

TOMAS PUSHED AWAY the food she'd brought. He didn't want
to be tempted by her at all—not her food, not her body, certainly not her smile.

He'd go for a workout and burn off the excess energy
making his blood race. He'd missed his usual session this
morning because he'd taken her to the market instead. It
had been a mistake. Discipline and routine were too important to toss aside so recklessly. He always worked out
in the morning because mornings were the worst for him.
At night he could go to bed with that little hope that he'd
wake up in the morning and his memories would be re-
stored and the nightmare would be over.

It never was.

Damn it. He pushed back his chair. He needed to go
burn out the self-pity.

Thing was, that usual agony hadn't lasted this morning.
Once he'd risen he'd been too busy anticipating her reaction to his farmers' market plan. And then she'd made him
stay with her. And it had been fun.

Too much fun.

He sighed as he set the treadmill to a faster pace and
harder angle than usual.

An hour later he walked in through the kitchen all hot
and sweaty but feeling better. Yet feeling bad too. He'd
been rude to her again and she didn't deserve it. He could
be civil until she left, couldn't he? Didn't she deserve that
little at least?

She glanced up from where she was stirring a pot on the

hob. The room smelt delicious. It was insane the way she could cook. Her gaze raked over him, that wariness in her eyes that he hated seeing. He'd been the one to put it there.

But to his surprise that dimple suddenly appeared and those sea-green eyes turned impish.

'You've not gone and turned that beautiful glasshouse into a home gym?' She arched her brows at him.

He was so pleased she was smiling, but still felt vaguely ashamed.

'You *haven't*.' She began to laugh at his expression, lightening the intensity of the atmosphere completely. 'It's so beautiful.'

'There might be a treadmill in there,' he conceded reluctantly, rubbing his hand through his hair, his chest aching—and not from the exercise.

She looked at him. 'And?'

'And a rowing machine.' A smile tugged at the corners of his mouth because she was too astute. 'And maybe a stationary bike.'

'Maybe?'

Her tease was too cute. And was just asking for retribution of the best kind.

'Maybe you should come and have a look at it,' he invited, fresh energy firing him. 'You shouldn't leave without seeing it.'

There was a moment of stillness as they both absorbed what he'd said and what it meant.

But then she lifted her head and her shoulders straightened. She looked him right in the eye. 'Then I'd love to see it.'

He held out his hand and she took it. Bittersweet peace settled within him as he walked with her along the snowy path through to the centre of the garden. The sun was setting, sending the last of its golden light through the masses of window panes.

'You're not cold?' She glanced at his shorts and tee.

'No.' Never around her. He stood back to let her go into the glasshouse first, then moved alongside so he could see her reaction.

'Oh. My.' Her jaw dropped.

He grinned, appreciating her incredulity. Pleasure rippled along his muscles, priming them for more.

'You've put a pool in.' She walked forward, gazing at it in frank admiration. *'Tomas...'*

He *really* liked the way she breathed his name like that. 'There was a pond, but we excavated it further. You like it?'

'I've never seen anything so beautiful.'

'So it's not an awful, boring home gym?'

She sent him a look. 'You know it isn't.'

'This is the only part of the estate I made significant changes to. I'm sure everyone will disapprove once they see it.'

'No, they won't,' she protested loudly. 'There are still all the beautiful plantings.' She stepped deeper into the verdant room. 'And the pool design is so sympathetic to the style of the building.' The Grecian-style marble looked as if it had been there for centuries. 'It really is just the perfect place for a party.' She sent him another look.

'You're not going to give up on trying to socialise me, are you?'

She giggled.

'I hate the thought of cocktail parties and polite chat,' he said bluntly.

'Are they too boring and shallow for a deep-thinking loner like you?'

He smiled at her sass and found himself being utterly honest.

'It's more the awkwardness of people knowing things that I don't. Things about myself. Things I've said and done that I have no recollection of. I hate them having that over me.' It made him feel weak, unable to hold his own and fight back. He loathed that feeling. He never wanted to feel that way again.

'So what?' She lifted a shoulder and let it drop in an expressive shrug. 'There's so much in general that I don't know about. I'm sure I always seem a fool. It's just too bad.'

He chuckled. 'I don't think so. You're inquisitive.'

'Yeah, well, we all know what happens to the curious cat.' She smiled wryly, but then sobered. 'I think if people knew about you, it would be awkward at first, but then…' She trailed off hopefully. 'They'd forget about it after a while. You're so smart and so up to date, you could converse on any subject better than most people ever could anyway.'

It was nice of her to say so, but it didn't change the incontrovertible. 'It's not possible, Zara.'

'Maybe in a while?'

She just wouldn't give up hope, would she?

She looked away from him back to the green foliage. 'I don't really like parties either,' she said softly.

'You're always in the kitchen?' He offered a weak joke.

'Pretty much.'

He didn't want this to get serious again. He wanted to escape with her for a little while longer. 'I guess we could have a pool party of our own.'

Her smile came back—sinful and sweet at the same time. 'I don't have my swimsuit with me.'

'No?' He reached out and wound his arm around her waist. 'Gosh, nor do I.' He mulled the problem with a *faux* serious expression. 'Whatever will we do?'

'Oh.' She smiled again as she caught his eye. 'I think you're a little bit wicked, Tomas Gallo.'

'Only a little bit?' He tugged her closer, enjoying the way she blossomed with him. It satisfied him in a way nothing else had. 'I'm going to have to work on that.'

His playfulness entranced her, seducing her all over again. But her heart ached at the same time. This was so fragile. So close to finished.

She forced herself to shut her mind from that imminent future. She'd make the most of this moment. It was almost all she had left.

'Promise me it's heated?' she asked as he deftly undid the fastening of her jeans.

'Of course.' He laughed again. 'The lengths aren't long, but the distance adds up and the weightlessness feels nice. It was to help my recovery.'

She nodded.

'You go first,' he dared as he released her.

'You want to watch me?' Surprise flooded her, followed swiftly by anticipation. And pleasure.

'Yes,' he admitted unashamedly.

He wanted to look at her. He liked to.

Well, *she* liked the way she affected him. That he took pleasure in her body pleased her. Because she very much liked looking at him.

She pushed her jeans down her legs and stepped out of them with a little shimmy.

He stood stock-still, his attention utterly focused on her.

'I've never skinny-dipped before,' she admitted shyly as she flung off her T-shirt and then unfastened her bra.

'So you're a bad influence,' she teased, bending to peel her panties down.

'I wouldn't say…' he breathed in deep as he looked at her '…bad.'

She blew him a little kiss and stepped towards the water. She slowly stepped in—to her ankles, her knees, her upper thighs. Then she stood still, her legs slightly apart.

It was warm, but not too hot, still refreshing on her super-sensitive skin. She glanced over her shoulder and saw he'd moved right to the edge, his hands on his hips as he kept his hot gaze trained on her. She cupped the water with her hands and lifted them to sprinkle some over her tight, bared breasts and down her belly. A little rivulet ran down from her navel. She shivered despite the civilised temperature of the water. There was nothing civilised about the need coiling deep within her. She arched her back a little as she repeated the water sprinkling. As the water trickled over her hot skin, she couldn't help rocking her hips. Back and forth. Back and forth.

'Zara?'

'Yes,' she breathed.

'Are you turning yourself on?'

'No.' Licking her lips, she faced him. 'You're doing that just by watching me.'

'Holy hell,' he muttered. 'You know you're a natural born seductress.'

She'd laugh if she weren't so aroused. 'What do you want me to do?'

He closed his eyes for a moment, clearly pulling himself together. 'Come here.'

'That's not going to be a problem.' She smiled at him impishly.

'Come here *now*.'

She dived, feeling the water wash over her hot body, then swam over to him. He took her by the hand and pulled her—not gently—from the pool.

'It seems impossible to believe there's snow outside when it's this steamy in here.' She ran a finger down his torso.

'Dare you to go out in it for a minute.'

'Stark naked?' She shook her head. 'You were the one all irate about me getting hypothermia a couple of days ago and there's far more snow out there now.'

'But I like warming you up again.'

'Then why aren't you?'

He looked slightly sheepish. 'I ought to rinse under the shower for a second.'

'Don't go anywhere,' she muttered. 'I want to look at you too. And I don't mind it when you're sweaty.'

She couldn't take her eyes off his body as he shrugged out of his shorts and tee. After his workout he seemed more ripped than ever—every muscle acutely defined and that sheen over his skin just emphasised it all the more.

'You don't mind my being a little…'

'Animal?' She planted a palm on his chest, loving how broad he was.

'You want to ride me?' he dared, a glint in his eye.

Her mouth dried. What had he just said? 'Um—'

'How is it you can still blush?' he softly teased. 'You want to take charge?'

She was steaming up on the inside now. But she pressed her hand against his mouth. 'Don't tempt me.'

'I live to tempt you,' he breathed against her fingers. 'So say anything. Do anything. Whatever you want. If you want to have your wicked way with me here on the floor, then I'll happily submit.'

'Oh, really?' She tried to tease him back. 'Because it would be such a sacrifice for you?'

He sighed theatrically. 'It might be hard to restrain myself, but for you I will try.'

'You'll just lie there and let me?' She didn't believe him; even that first time when he'd pulled her astride him, he'd still really led their dance.

'I'll lie there for as long as I can.'

Her eyes narrowed as she recognised the caveat in his promise. 'In other words, you'll take over when you want to.'

His smile widened. 'Probably.'

She'd almost run out of time. There was only now. So

she was taking and making it hers. Making *him* hers. 'Then you'd better get down on that floor.'

'I think you're a little bit wicked too, Zara Falconer.'

'Not as wicked as you.' She shook her head. 'You can have me any time and you know it.'

'The same goes for you so I guess we're even.'

He was wrong about that. She was going to take full advantage because she knew this was going to be the last time. It had to be purely physical. Not emotional. Nothing more than a simple delight.

Except there was this humour they shared, this fun.

'If you're that wild,' he muttered, a gleam in his eye as she moved to kneel astride him, 'why don't you try riding a little higher? I could lick that trail of water from you.'

Heat washed over her body as she skimmed her fingertips up his chest. 'What?'

'You heard.' His hands gripped her waist, pulling her upwards, towards his chest. His face. His lips curved into the sexiest smile she'd ever seen. And his eyes gleamed like onyx.

'You're—'

'Tempting you.'

Oh, he was. So very much. Holding his gaze, she moved that bit further up his body. Sensing his victory, he wrapped his arms around her thighs, holding her wide.

Oh, it was scandalously intimate. It was also the most blatantly erotic moment of her life. She rocked her hips gently and he lifted his head a little to catch her with sweeps of his tongue. With kisses that grew hungrier and more powerful. She groaned, writhing as he thrilled her. But just before she came, she pulled away—teasing herself as much as him.

He growled in protest, but said nothing. A calculating gleam entered his eye as she kissed her way down his body.

'My shorts pocket,' he muttered.

'It's okay,' she said. 'I have one in my jeans.'

His little laugh pleased her. His muffled oath as she tried to sheath him pleased her too.

'Have mercy,' he muttered, pushing her hands out of the way in the end. 'Let me do it before I lose it too soon.'

She knew she probably wasn't going to last long once she started properly on him, so she paused to look up at the patterned glass ceiling high above her. 'This is truly beautiful.'

'Yes.'

She shot him a look. 'Flattery will get you everywhere.'

'It's not flattery.' He reached up and tweaked her nipple. 'Are you really looking at the scenery at this exact moment?'

She laughed as she looked down at the strain in his body as he waited for her to stake her claim. 'Am I taking too long?'

'You're killing me.'

'Well, we can't have that,' she teased.

But her laughter died as she slid down on him, finally taking him to the hilt.

'Hell, Zara.'

She looked into his eyes as they both paused to savour that moment. Suddenly it was nothing *but* emotional. He knew how amazing he could make her feel. How incredible she found making love with him. That was what this was for her—she was making love to him as freely as she could this final day.

She tried to ride him fast, but in the end all she felt was frantic. She abandoned the attempt altogether, reaching forward to kiss him. She needed to kiss him so badly. He gripped her shoulders, holding her to him and meeting her mouth with as much passion as she felt. The orgasm almost took her by surprise, hitting as she simply lay over him, on him, ground as close as she could get. No fierce thrusting, or playful fingers pressing the point above where they joined. Just kissing and straining connection. And she was there.

Home with him.

'It really is getting too cold out here, Sleeping Beauty.' Tomas bent low and scooped his sleepy lover into his arms.

Her eyes finally flashed open. 'You can't carry me all that way.'

'Don't think you can tell me what I can and can't do.' Tomas hoisted her higher in her arms just to prove the point.

'As if you don't try to do that to me.' She rubbed her cheek against his chest as he carried her across the snowy path and into the big house.

'I've discovered my latent desire to be a naturist,' he said as he set her down inside the warm kitchen. 'There's nothing better than walking around this house with you completely bare. I might have to hide all your clothes and you'll have to stay naked always.'

'Could be dangerous while cooking,' she answered tartly. 'I wouldn't want to get burned somewhere personal.'

'No.' He leaned close. 'We wouldn't want that.' He kissed her and found his lust resurging. 'The only marks on this body should be made by my mouth.'

She shivered as he bent to her breasts.

'Only from pleasure,' he added.

'You're insatiable.' But she moaned as she said it.

'I'm merely trying to keep up with you.' He laughed with arrogant satisfaction as she wriggled that little bit closer, wanting him to resume his teasing touch. 'So very demanding.'

But he was every bit as needy as she. He simply couldn't resist any more. He bent his head to kiss her again. The beast in him liked to make a mark on her. To brand her as his in a deeply personal, physical way, so the world would know that she was his. That only he had the right to touch her most privately.

He was in trouble and he knew it. But he was too far gone to stop now. One more night. Just one more. He couldn't bite back the growl of satisfaction as she arched towards him, angling her head so he could keep suckling the tender skin of her neck.

He knew she liked it too.

With a groan he bent his head and succumbed to his appetite, consigning that nagging concern to the back of his brain while his body—his soul—was sated. Despite that fear of impending disaster, he didn't think he was ever going to get enough.

CHAPTER ELEVEN

How sorry she was.

HER CONSCIENCE STABBED her awake, but it was centuries till dawn. She counted the slow minutes as she waited for a more reasonable hour to wake him. She ought to do it now. Wake him and tell him. Apologise over and over. But it was the first night he'd not left to go to his room and he was in such a restful sleep and she couldn't bear to just yet.

The room slowly lightened. He'd left a chink in the heavy curtains to let the starlight gleam in and eventually a beam of sunlight lit a bar across the bed.

Secretly, silently, she gazed at him, indulging for a last moment and telling herself she wasn't really a stalker. A year ago she'd thought she'd fallen in love with him—that man who'd walked into her life and tipped it upside down before walking out again just over twenty-four hours later. He'd been her shining knight. The man who'd helped her escape misery. But she'd been so naive. In these last few days she'd got to know him for real—his humour, his struggles, his truth. There was so much more to love than just that gorgeous, scarred exterior. He was so much more complicated, more human than that beautiful bone structure and roguish charm.

She froze as he stirred.

His eyes opened and he blinked sleepily. She braced, strengthening her aching heart, knowing she had to do it now. She saw the moment he completely wakened. Awareness sharpened his eyes and for a half-second that frown appeared. But then he smiled and a look entered those eyes that melted her heart. But not her resolve.

But before she could speak he lifted up onto his elbow and leaned over to kiss her. Heaven help her, she couldn't deny herself—or him—that kiss.

But that kiss led to another. Then another. And then he covered her. Wordless, worshipping, it was the gentlest of possessions. His arms were strong but tender bars as he held her. Oh, she couldn't resist this last moment of absolute joy. She wanted to give him everything.

It wasn't a frantic, passionate coupling but this was no less demanding. If anything, it was more so. She was wound unbearably tight, her body aching for more. Each slow, deep thrust was the most exquisite torment.

He looked into her eyes as he pressed closer, still too deliciously slow. She couldn't cope with the intensity. Her body taut as a bowstring, she strained to kiss him, to show him how sorry she was, how much she cared, how much she wanted. His pace finally quickened. His teeth nipped her lips as she neared the peak, sending her higher in a sudden rush. Her orgasm collided with his into that timeless moment of shared ecstasy. She clutched him closer still, yearning that it would last for ever. But it was a moment that, like all, slipped from her grasp.

And so did he.

She barely heard the words he whispered as she sank into the dark depths of exhaustion.

'I like waking up to you.'

When she woke the second time the sun was much higher in the sky. She sat bolt upright in the bed. She was alone and heartsick. But she heard noises from along the corridor. *Voices.*

She leapt from the bed. Cold sweat slicked her body and her pulse scurried. Quickly she tugged on jeans and a T-shirt as she remembered that sweetly whispered confession from such a carefully guarded soul.

'I like waking up to you.'

It was the nearest to a declaration of affection he'd probably ever give. And she'd made such a mistake by being such a coward.

So much for thinking that she'd developed as a person. For so long she'd been silent—willing to put up with misery because she was too scared to take any kind of risk. And she'd thought she'd moved on from that. She'd studied. She'd taken a small bedsit on her own. She was developing her business and had had some success with it already...but at her first real chance to prove her strength, she'd failed.

She'd taken the easy way out. By doing nothing. Saying nothing. Being silent and passive and pretending she was doing the right thing.

But it was *her* responsibility to be honest with Tomas. She was the one who'd entered into that marriage with him. She was the one who had benefited. But she'd hidden behind Jasper, not wanting to face up to the consequences herself.

Not face up to the truth.

If Tomas hadn't had the accident, the truth was she'd most likely never have seen him again in her whole life. Their marriage had been little more than a joke to him. A cavalier moment of chivalry that he'd probably not thought twice about since. It had been a way of giving her money and setting her free.

In anyone else it would have been an extreme action, but for Tomas Gallo—it had been a piece of calculated retaliation and risk with the reward for her. A transaction her uncle couldn't argue with and that soothed her pride at the same time.

She thought she understood a little more now why he'd done it. And that flash of maverick outrageousness was some of what she loved about him. Beneath the ruthless businessman, there was scarring and old, old wounds. But

he'd not become embittered, there was kindness and gener-
osity in him. He was a man who played the game his way.

Only his way.

But he would not be pleased to know she'd kept this
from him. He might not be forgiving. His pride was part of
his desire for isolation—he did not like to be made a fool
of. But more importantly, more deep, was the distrust he
had of people. Of relationships. Of 'family'. She was his
family now.

And she had let him down terribly.

But she had no time to waste because if that was Jasper,
she had to get to Tomas before he said anything.

She swiftly ran to his office. She'd never felt as cold as
she did in that moment. The two men were standing on the
other side of Tomas's large desk. Jasper looked as dapper
as ever in his grey three-piece suit, but it was Tomas, clad
completely in black again, with his shirt sleeves rolled to
just below the elbows, who commanded all her attention.

He glanced up the second she'd made it to the doorway.
The look in his eyes was enough to render her immobile.
There were papers spread on the desk. Official-looking
forms.

Her heart stopped.

'Jasper,' she said breathlessly, but she couldn't tear her
gaze from Tomas.

He knew.

'Zara,' Jasper said with too much joviality. 'You're looking well.'

She was looking as if she'd just gotten out of bed after
a sleepless night of seduction. Which she had. But she was
too afraid of Tomas's reaction to this news to blush. Sickened, she still couldn't move.

The awkward atmosphere grew.

'He's told you,' she whispered, forcing herself to break
the silence.

'Told me what?' Tomas prompted in staccato tones.
'That…'

'What has Jasper come all this way to tell me, Zara?'

'Now, Tom—'

'Zara can tell me.' Tomas cut Jasper off without releasing her from his imprisoning gaze. 'Can't you, Zara?'

He was going to make her say it after all. And wasn't that fair enough?

Tears sprang to her eyes and a hard lump of emotion clogged her throat. Such regret. But she swallowed it back. She refused to look away and fail. Not now. Even when it was too late.

She drew in a harsh breath, determined to get her voice stronger than a weak whisper. 'That we've met before. That you once helped me.'

'I helped you,' he echoed, still in those staccato, undeniably angry tones. 'How did I do that, exactly?'

'You married me.'

She saw his eyes widen as she put the truth into words. He was furious; she could feel his anger coming at her in waves.

'You—'

'Tomas,' Jasper interrupted sharply.

Tomas whirled to face him. 'You. Leave. Now.'

'Tomas—'

'Go look at the goddamn garden.' He silenced the older man.

Jasper hesitated and looked searchingly at Zara.

'Don't worry, I'm not about to go crazy and attack her. She's in no danger from the damaged—'

'Jasper, it's okay,' Zara interrupted Tomas. She needed to speak to him alone.

Jasper walked past her, his eyes sharpening on her as he neared. It was a silent query that she met with something as near to a smile as she could muster.

Then she stood silent, waiting for Tomas to vent.

He waited until Jasper was well out of earshot. But it wasn't a shout, it was a very soft single question. He barely even moved his mouth, but she heard it as if he'd hollered it through a megaphone.

'Why?'

'Why what?' she asked, bravely walking towards him.

'Why did we marry? Why didn't I tell you?'

'Why are you here?'

She breathed out. That was the easiest of all the questions. 'Jasper thought it might help. That seeing me might spur your memory.'

'And sleeping with me would help too? Did you discuss that idea with him?'

'Of course not. That just…'

'Just what?'

'Just happened.'

He looked sceptical. 'Because you felt sorry for me? Did you sacrifice your virginity to say thank you?'

'I—' She broke off. It had been no sacrifice. Her anger began to build. 'As I told you before, I slept with you because I wanted you. And because I care about you.'

He laughed. A bitter, disbelieving mockery of a laugh that scalded her like acid. She'd told him the truth and he'd laughed at her.

He sat down behind his desk. She stood on the other side of it, feeling as if she'd been summoned to the boss's office for a bawling out.

Which was pretty much the case.

'Who are you really?'

'I'm exactly who I said I was. Zara Falconer.'

His expression didn't change.

'I've been studying at a cookery school up north. I sell my cakes and biscuits at a local market—that was how Jasper tracked me down.'

'Before that. Tell me everything that happened between us. From the beginning.'

She swallowed. 'There's not that much to tell. You and Jasper had been on a business trip to Antigua in the Caribbean. To look at my uncle's casino operation amongst other things. You had a business meeting on his yacht. That's where you met me.'

'And this was the uncle you lived with after your parents died?'

'I'd lived on that boat for almost a decade.' She nodded.

'How is it possible that you couldn't just leave of your own accord?'

She looked at the floor. She understood how it sounded. She was a grown woman. Why couldn't she just have given her uncle the finger, walked out of the door and not looked back? There were no chains holding her there...but then there were. Invisible chains that hurt in their own vindictive way.

'When someone tells you you're worthless, day in and out...several times a day. When you've been transplanted from your home, your country and you're isolated from your old friends...and the only people you have around you are the ones telling you to be grateful. So grateful because without them you'd have nothing. That you *are* nothing...'

She forced herself to try to explain. 'I had no money of my own. No job. No training. I had no idea how to get out of there. Most of the time I was literally stuck on a boat in the middle of the ocean. He had my passport and was the trustee of what little money my parents had left me...'

That had all gone. He'd said they'd needed it for her expenses.

'I was so shy. I tried, but I was so afraid of doing everything wrong.' And she had done lots wrong—worn the wrong thing, said the wrong thing. She'd retreated more and more, hiding below deck.

She'd processed it since, worked it through. But all those years of isolation had left their mark; the shadow lingered.

'My uncle was determined to impress you. He thought you were a prospective investor. He'd always had plans to expand his casino. He was so angry when I served you at your meeting. He made jokes at my expense. You smiled, seemed to go along with them…' But then she'd looked at him surreptitiously and had caught him looking at her. That moment that he'd held her gaze then? 'But you told him you weren't going to invest. He was very angry but hid it from you.' She drew in a shaky breath. 'He didn't hide it from me.'

She paused, hating having to relive this, hoping that Tomas could see she was speaking the truth. If only she'd told him sooner.

'You overheard him,' she muttered. 'You saw the mark on my cheek. And you asked if I wanted to get out.'

'So I bought you?'

'That's how my uncle saw it.' Because he'd viewed her as a chattel. 'And he didn't hesitate to let you. You framed it as part of the business deal. It was only afterwards that you told him you'd never ever invest in his company. And that he was never to come after me or ask me for money. That if he did you'd destroy his business and his reputation by telling the world he'd basically sold his niece. He's not contacted me since.'

'And that's what you wanted?'

'I changed my name the minute I could to prevent him from finding me.'

'That was why Jasper couldn't find you sooner?'

'Yes. He spotted a piece about me in my local papers. It was about my cakes at the market and there was a photo with it. I guess he thought it was worth a shot.'

'How much did I give you?'

'You offered me a million as our annulment settlement.

I took ten thousand. I have just less than half of it. I'm still saving to repay the amount in full. The money you gave me enabled my escape, but it was your ability to pull it off that just...' She couldn't explain it. Her confidence in him had given her confidence in herself. He had made such a difference to her. He'd never truly understand it.

And from the look on his face, he didn't even want to try.

'Your uncle's picture is upstairs in the gallery?' he asked sharply.

'Yes.'

'But not yours.'

'No.'

He breathed out.

'I don't think you ever had a picture. And there was no record...'

'Jasper had a record. *You* knew.'

'But I didn't know about your amnesia. I'd read about your accident, of course—' She broke off. 'But all the reports said you'd made a full recovery. And I thought the annulment had gone through.'

'So then you came here and after all I'd done, you lied to me.'

'I didn't lie.'

'You told me we hadn't met.'

'I said you didn't know me. And you didn't.'

'Semantics,' he spat. 'You omitted vitally important information. I don't care if you thought it was for the best, it was wrong. It was especially wrong to sleep with me while withholding that information.'

But if she'd told him, he wouldn't have slept with her. And yes, now she realised she'd been so desperate. She was still desperate.

'Back that day, I thought I was in love with you,' she said, her breath seizing. 'Love at first sight, even though you didn't really see me at all. I knew you weren't really interested in me. It was just because my uncle's behaviour annoyed you so much. But now I realise that, all this time, what I felt was just a huge crush. You came along when I was so trapped and you were like this flash of lightning. So bright. So mesmerising. And you got me out of there. How could I ever look at any other man?'

She swallowed.

'So, yes, when Jasper said to come and see you I couldn't resist.' She moved towards the window, trying to summon the courage to keep speaking as honestly. 'When you didn't recognise me at first I thought it was just because... I hadn't been anything important to you. Then I worked it out.'

'So you're over your crush now?' he asked so dryly her heart almost shrivelled.

'Yes,' she answered softly. She held her hands tightly together, her fingers twisting into each other. 'I'm out of the crush and fully in love with you.'

'You think you're in love with me?' he scoffed bitterly. 'You've fallen for a fantasy. The Prince Charming who rescued you that one day. It's not real. It'll never be real. I'm not that guy and I never will be.'

'No, I know you now.' She fought back the tears. She'd never been so exposed.

'What do you think you know? *I* don't know who I am, so how the hell can you know anything?'

'I know the man you are, the things you do. The way you treat people—me. I know you're strong and determined and loyal. You're arrogant as hell but kind with it. *How* you are is *who* you are. And you're so much more than the man who rescued me.'

And she was more than the wraith of a person who'd needed that in the first place.

He stared at her for a long moment. 'There is nothing between us,' he said matter-of-factly. 'This was a fun few days. It's been a while since I've had a woman in my bed. You were here. It was convenient. But we're finished.'

Anger bubbled deep in her belly. Was he really going to play this that way—after everything she'd told him? Everything she'd tried to show him?

She walked towards him. 'So that's it—I made a mistake and you're saying it's all over?'

'It was always going to be over,' he said bluntly. 'When the Kilpatricks come back you'd leave and we'd be done. You knew that was the deal. Now I just have to hope that you won't sell your story.'

'I haven't yet,' she threw back at him angrily.

'But we both know you'll sell anything you have to when you need money.'

She gasped. 'You *offered*,' she said in a fierce voice. 'I took less than you offered. And I was always going to pay you back.' She'd started a savings account for that purpose already. And one of the reasons she'd come here in the first place was to pay him back.

'Consider your virginity as full and final payment.'

Oh, that was cruel. 'People make mistakes every single day, Tomas. And other people forgive them.'

'Some things are unforgivable.'

'Was wanting you so very awful of me?' She flared up at him. 'Was it so terrible to care? To want not to hurt you? Was being attracted to you such a terrible sin?'

'You're confusing gratitude with desire.'

'Give me some credit.'

'Why should I?'

'You know what?' she asked as she lost control of her emotions. 'You didn't die in that accident, but you're barely living now.' Her anger spilled over. 'I don't understand it. Don't you of all people know how fleeting and precious life can be? But you've trapped yourself here and you're so bitter—'

'Don't I have a right to be?' he snapped back at her.

'Of course. To a point. But not for ever. You're letting pride get in the way of having a full life—'

'I don't want this from you. I don't want you for anything more than what I've had. I didn't then and I don't now.' He strode towards her, his fury frothing as the words tumbled from his mouth. 'All this was was sex. When you were offering everything why wouldn't I take it? But it means nothing. I don't need you or anyone to make my life complete.'

'Fine,' she said. 'Lock yourself away here for ever. Lie to yourself and think you're happy making your pots of money so you can be safe and hide away for ever. Be lonely and grumpy and isolated and miserable.'

'I *am* happy here. How can I not be?' He swept his arms wide.

'With everything covered in dust cloths and left unused?' she cried at him. 'You could have so much more. You *deserve* so much more.'

He halted a few paces away from her. The anger in his eyes suddenly died, but the expression that replaced it was even worse. It was a deadening of all emotion, until he was simply a blank.

'You realise I can't trust a word you say,' he said quietly, his words striking like mortal blows. 'And I will never be able to.'

CHAPTER TWELVE

'I don't want to leave.'

JASPER WAS MAKING a muddy track as he paced back and forth on the wet lawn. Tomas bit back his anger as he stalked up to him. He'd had to get away from Zara. He needed to get away from them both.

'Don't be angry with her,' Jasper said as soon as he saw Tomas walking towards him. 'It was my idea. She didn't know any of it.'

'Didn't know she was my wife?'

As if he could believe that.

'Not until the day she got here, no.' Jasper puffed out a breath. 'She thought the annulment had gone through a year ago. I didn't tell her about the amnesia when I met her again. I'd hoped your seeing her might jolt your memory.'

'Why would that happen when I'd spent only a day in her presence?' It was preposterous.

Jasper ran his hand through his hair and coughed. 'Because...'

'Because what?'

'You married her, for God's sake,' he muttered. 'You, who never dated anyone for more than a month or so, took one look at this little mouse and married her. I was gobsmacked.'

'Apparently it was to help her.'

'It was.' Jasper nodded. 'And she needed it. But there was more to it than that.'

'What?'

'I saw the way you kissed her.'

Tomas's eyes narrowed. He hadn't kissed Zara since Jasper had arrived this morning. 'When did you see that?' He straightened. 'When I was allowed to "kiss the bride"?' It would have been for show.'

Jasper shook his head. 'You didn't kiss at the ceremony. It was afterwards. When you went to say goodbye to her. I was along the hallway and you...'

'What?'

'It was...' Jasper cleared his throat awkwardly. 'That's why when I found her I sent her to you. She's the only person you've ever reacted to in that way. You kissed her. Hell, you kissed her like—'

'You forget yourself,' Tomas snapped. 'You're my lawyer, not my friend. Stay out of my personal life, Jasper. Never, ever interfere like this again. Be very grateful you've not been sacked this second.'

'You asked me to hold off on filing the annulment papers,' Jasper said quickly. 'I don't know why, but you did. We went to Paris for your next series of meetings and then the accident happened.' Jasper lifted his hands in a helpless gesture.

And it was helpless; he was hopeless. He could never know the truth for certain. He could never trust her.

Tomas went back indoors and took the stairs two at a time. He needed them both gone from his home.

Now.

There was a wildness in his eyes but every movement was so controlled, he was like burning ice. Zara rubbed her arms as she watched him coolly sign the annulment papers.

He didn't speak, he didn't look at her. Just through her.

Destroyed inside, she followed his lead and signed, then dated the papers. She needed to talk to him again, to try to make him understand, but he wasn't going to give her that chance.

'I can give you a ride somewhere if you'd like me to,

Zara?' Jasper stood with his back to Tomas, as if he knew he was risking the wrath of his employer.

'My car—'

'Is in the village,' Tomas interrupted. 'It's been fixed. Jasper can drop you off and you can pick it up on your way through. It's been paid for.' He glanced at his desk. 'The Kilpatricks don't get back until Tuesday but I think I can cope alone for a couple of days.'

Zara winced; could he sound any more sarcastic?

'Is that okay with you, Zara?' Jasper asked.

She tried to hide her tumbling emotions. The older man was concerned, so she smiled. 'I think it's a good idea.'

She wanted time to talk to Tomas. To make him understand. But he wasn't allowing that. He was sending her away.

'You'd better pack,' Tomas muttered in her direction without looking at her. 'And you concentrate on getting those papers filed as quickly as possible,' he ordered Jasper. 'Leave everything else for me to sort out.'

He didn't speak to her again.

It took less than five minutes for her to put her clothes into her bag. She was so very cold. So hurt. And hopeless.

Tomas stood in the doorway, a forbidding expression on his face as he watched Jasper get into his car. She saw no way of breaking through to him.

She gazed up at him, at an even greater disadvantage height wise because she was on the lower step, trying not to slip in the melting snow.

But she had to take one last chance. One last risk.

'I don't want to leave,' she pleaded softly.

Finally he turned and looked directly at her, that dead look still dulling his expression. 'If you stayed, it would only be to have sex and I don't want you any more.'

CHAPTER THIRTEEN

It was always going to be just out of reach.

TOMAS COULDN'T BELIEVE the day had ended so horrendously.

For the first time since the accident he'd woken up happy. Yes, he'd had that moment when he'd remembered what he'd lost, but then he'd opened his eyes and looked straight into hers.

It wasn't just his body that had responded. His very soul had lifted. The loss had diminished, ebbing away like a gentle tide and taking the usual frustration and bitterness with it. It hadn't mattered because *she'd* been by his side. She'd smiled at him, her eyes luminous and—he'd thought—loving.

Waking up next to her had been the best moment of his life in so very long. He'd actually dared to think he might have found something he'd not thought possible. He'd thought he could hold onto it.

But it was all a charade.

She'd fooled herself into thinking she was in love with him. It was some hideous mix of pity and gratitude. And, yes, sexual attraction.

But not love.

It was as if the sweetest of cakes had crumbled to ash in his mouth.

And as for the veracity of her tale? He could well believe he'd played the hero in a moment of madness—one look into those dreamy eyes and he'd have done almost anything she'd asked.

But he was damned if he was going to shackle her to him and a life of servitude that she'd really only just escaped.

She'd done nice things for him because it was how she could show her appreciation. All those touches had been about saying thank you, more than anything else.

It hurt. He felt like a damned fool. A weak, vulnerable idiot.

Well, no more of that. He'd get back to work. Properly focus. Keep the company pushing forward.

He'd forget all about her.

But in the cruellest irony of all, his brain refused to block the memory of her with him. All he could think about was Zara. All he could see was the devastated expression in her eyes when he'd rejected her.

When he'd banished her.

He closed his eyes and willed himself to move forward. To concentrate. To do anything but ruminate over the last few days events. But it was futile. Time and time again his thoughts turned to her.

And the ache in his chest?

He pushed through, determinedly firing off email after email. Demanding reports come back to him sooner. Researching to find a new trend. Anything to occupy his mind.

It was almost midnight when he stalked into his room and slammed the door shut. Thank heavens he hadn't taken her into his own bed and tainted it with memories of her there.

But he couldn't sleep. At who knew what hour he found himself walking back down the corridor, to the room she'd slept in and walking into it. There was barely a sign of her presence. Only the faintest lingering lemony fragrance.

He sat on the edge of the bed and breathed in the pain.

Maybe she was right. Maybe it *was* pride holding him captive here. Maybe he was afraid of showing any kind of vulnerability because he knew this was such a dog-eat-dog world. Every man for himself and all that. He'd lived it, breathed it, built his empire on the rules he knew governed it. Money made a man. People had power over those who were poor and vulnerable and he wasn't putting himself at risk again. He couldn't when it had taken so much to claw his way out of that position.

And even if what she felt for him was genuine? Even if she really was in love with him?

His rejection of her wasn't about him at all. It was about what was best for *her*. He couldn't be the man she deserved to have. She didn't need someone who might let her down. He couldn't be everything she needed. He didn't know from one day to the next whether he'd wake up and remember anything at all any more. He wasn't lumbering her with that. Not when she'd fought so long and so hard to get herself free from the oppression and emotional burden of her uncle. She wasn't becoming his *caretaker*. It was never, ever happening.

He wasn't what was best for her. He never would be.

And he couldn't bear the thought of losing this too— these precious new memories.

At some point he slept—still dressed and on the edge of the bed he'd shared with her. When he woke, it was the worst moment ever. Furious with his inability to rationalise, he went out to the glasshouse, determined to maintain his daily routine. He worked out—longer and harder than usual.

Then he stomped to the kitchen. He hadn't eaten in hours. The lights were off and it was cold. There'd been no warm woman up baking at two in the morning making the whole house smell scrumptious and making him smile with her enthusiasm. And it was silent. She'd taken her phone and its relentlessly upbeat playlist with her.

But she'd left him reminders. He lifted the lid from the container he found in the fridge. There was a cake in there. A typically Zara, lemon-loaded, generously proportioned cake. He couldn't help it, his mouth watered. He cut a piece and put it on a plate and took a seat at the table that now held such significance. He bit into the treat.

As he'd known—feared—it was too delicious for anyone's good. And as he chewed, it came. That fleeting moment of familiarity—remembrance. But the returning memory remained just out of reach.

It was always going to be just out of reach. Eternally elusive.

Déjà vu again, tormenting him, because his brain now knew he'd met her before and it was trying to piece it together.

He was never going to remember any of that day he'd first met her. The day he'd married her. He'd done something so extreme and he couldn't remember a thing about it. He couldn't remember her at all. How was that *possible*?

He stood in fury and threw the plate into the sink.

The sound of it smashing echoed in his head as he stalked out of the room.

In his office the empty entries in his journal tortured him more. He flicked through the last couple of pages. Then he flicked back further, determined to remind himself of what was important.

His business. His privacy. Priorities, right?

Except as he flicked through the pages, he couldn't find what he was looking for. He tossed the journal down in exasperation. It was the most boring thing he'd read in months. He, who supposedly had an aptitude for identifying patterns, was only just seeing the reality now. His life had become so constrained and isolated—and boring. And he'd thought he was happy...but he wasn't.

He'd never been more miserable. Not even that day when the specialist told him his memory might never return was as bad as this. Because only now did he understand what he'd done to himself. And to her.

His fear of losing more had meant he was too afraid to live in the present.

It wasn't that he couldn't trust Zara. He couldn't trust *himself.* His worst fear was that he'd lose more of his memory and become a millstone around her neck.

He'd told himself it was just lust, just a case of having a beautiful woman under his nose for the first time in for ever—exactly the insecurity she'd once voiced. And as he'd replied, that idea was an insult to her. And to him.

It was only to her that he'd had such a reaction. It would only ever be to her.

And here he was afraid again—unable to trust that she hadn't done what she had out of some misguided sense of obligation and pity. But wasn't that insulting her all over again? Was he really going to believe that she didn't know her own mind? She'd told him as much herself—she hadn't given up her virginity to him out of pity. She'd wanted him. Plain and simple. And she'd had him. Exactly the way he'd wanted her himself. And he wanted more too.

Now he hoped she still wanted him—for more than just his body.

If he didn't earn her pity any more—by stopping hiding and starting to live—then maybe they could be together as equals.

But he had to stop hiding now.

Because he hadn't only lost his past. He'd stalled his present. And he'd lost his future too. He'd pushed her out of the door and slammed it after her.

He was an absolute idiot.

CHAPTER FOURTEEN

It was a lie.

ZARA GASPED AS she read the headline that dominated the online newspaper. She sank into the chair as her legs weakened and she squinted and leaned closer to the screen to read further.

Galloway Investments CEO suffers
severe memory loss

Tomas Gallo, millionaire CEO of Galloway Investments, was the victim of a near-fatal collision a year ago. Sources close to Gallo say the accident left his memory impaired with a temporal amnesia and there is no likelihood of full recovery. Yet the business has thrived, with Galloway Investments providing more than a twenty per cent return to investors in the last twelve months.

Sources say his work output has not been diminished at all. The CEO, always known for his work ethic, has become reclusive since the accident, living alone in an estate in Buckinghamshire. He is rarely seen in public.

She skimmed the accompanying fact box explaining his kind of amnesia and more about the company's stellar results but her gaze leapt back to that awful headline. Her blood iced.

This was terrible. This was exactly what Tomas hadn't wanted. And for it to have been leaked less than a week since she'd left him? There'd be no prizes for guessing who he'd suspect. Panicking, she grabbed her phone and hit Jasper's number. She'd not spoken to him at all in the five days since he'd dropped her into the village to collect her car. And the only conversation they'd had then was apology met with apology.

'How did they find out?' she asked as soon as Jasper answered. 'Who betrayed him?'

Who was the 'close source' who'd told all about his head injury?

'Have you spoken with him?' she added before Jasper had the chance to answer. 'Is he okay?'

'I haven't been able to contact him today,' Jasper finally answered in his usual cautious manner.

Zara pressed her hand to her forehead.

'He'll be all right, Zara,' the lawyer added calmly.

Probably, but 'all right' wasn't enough. He was unhappier than he'd ever admit. He was isolated and lonely and determined to believe he liked it that way and she feared this exposure would only drive him deeper into his seclusion. But he had so much to offer and she hated the thought of him being alone in that huge house all the time when he should be laughing and teasing and *loved*. There was so much in him to love.

'Are you going to see him?' she demanded.

'I can't. I'm en route to the airport now. I have a meeting to get to in New York.'

Jasper was going to the States *now*? 'You don't think checking on him is more important?'

'His company is important to him, Zara,' Jasper said firmly. 'It's what he's told me to do.'

'So ignore what he's told you and go check on him,' she snapped.

'I value my job and I respect Tomas. If he says he can handle it, he can handle it.'

That wasn't good enough. It wasn't okay to leave him alone when this news had just broken.

'I've already crossed the line with sending you there in the first place,' Jasper suddenly explained in a chastened tone. 'My job is to take care of the company, not the man.'

'But you care about the man.'

'Of course I do,' he replied. 'I care about him enough to do as he's instructed without argument.'

But what Tomas was asking was pure defensive reflex— putting his company ahead of his personal life as he'd always done. This was only going to drive him deeper into his isolated world.

'How are you doing, Zara?'

Her heart stalled at the gentle pity in Jasper's query. Of course he knew how she felt about Tomas; there'd been no hiding how devastated she'd been when he'd made her leave the other morning. She'd been almost silent in that car, but there'd been tears she couldn't stop from falling.

'I'm fine,' she assured Jasper quickly, glancing around her dreary little bedsit. 'It was a rough week and this was a shock, but I'm okay. I've been very busy getting back into my work.'

It was a lie. She'd spent the first two days crying. Then she'd pulled herself together and told herself to get on with it. But it was damn hard. She missed him with every fibre of her being.

She ended the call as quickly as she could, still angry and upset and still none the wiser about who had betrayed Tomas's confidence.

Jasper might be willing to say yes to everything Tomas wanted, but she wasn't going to. She was going to stand up and do what she knew in her heart was right.

He might not feel the same way about her, and that was fine, but she could check on him as a friend. And the only way she was going to know he was okay was to see him face to face. And she needed him to know she hadn't been the one to expose him. Honestly, she just ached to see him.

Decision made, she threw her bag into the car and locked up her small bedsit.

The entire drive down she mentally planned what she was going to say, envisaging how he might react. He'd probably changed the security code and she wouldn't even get past the gate. But if that happened she'd just have to climb it.

Almost four hours of non-stop driving later, she pulled up at the heavy gates. Her legs were stiff as she got out of the car and she stretched to ease them. She punched the security code and waited that half-moment.

'Miss, miss!'

She turned at the voice, startled to see a man with a large camera peering out from a gap in the hedge.

'Are you here to see Tomas, miss?'

As he asked he took photos of her as she stood, stunned and immobile. And then she heard that familiar creaking of the gates opening.

Galvanised into action, she dashed back to her car and drove through the gates, hoping the man wouldn't try to follow her in. Nervously she checked the rear-view mirror but to her relief saw he'd remained on the other side of the gates. But he was still taking photos of her.

Good Lord, it was horrendous.

She tried to pull her focus back and remember how she'd planned to greet Tomas, but all she could think was how relieved she was that it wasn't raining and that she wouldn't look as bedraggled as she had that first night she'd arrived here.

As she parked the car in front of the big house her heart sank. The beautiful building looked empty and cold and she knew he wasn't home. She wasn't surprised he'd left, given there were paparazzi stalking him.

She knocked on the door regardless, hoping the house-keeper might be in, but no one answered. Deflated after driving all that way, she leaned back against the gleaming black door and stared down the driveway. She wasn't sure what to do next. She didn't want to drive back out past that photographer. She didn't want to leave without seeing Tomas.

She'd just have to wait. She slid down the door and sat at the base of it, wrapping her arms around her knees so she was in a tight little ball. She'd wait as long as it took.

But it was only about twenty minutes later when she heard shouting and the faint clang of the gates in the distance. She scrambled to her feet as a car came round the corner of the driveway. Without thinking she walked to the edge of the top step. Her breathing quickened as she recognised the vehicle as Tomas's big grey four-wheel-drive. As it drew closer she saw he was alone in the car, his expression hidden behind sunglasses. He parked it right behind hers, so it blocked her exit, preventing her from leaving in any great hurry.

She held her breath as he stepped out of the car. There were tired lines in his face, stubble on his jaw, yet there was energy in his leashed movements as he walked towards her. He removed his sunglasses and his gaze burned her skin with that hot accusation—like the time he'd caught her watching him from the window. He was heart-stoppingly gorgeous. But her heart jack-hammered as she realised how angry he was.

'I—I didn't tell anyone—' she stammered immediately, thinking of the paparazzi hounding him at the gate. 'It wasn't me.'

'I know.' He stopped on the bottom step, meaning his face was almost level with hers.

'Honestly, I—' She broke off. He'd believed her?

'I know it wasn't you,' he repeated, his almost black eyes unfathomable and unwavering. 'Is that why you're here?'

'I—' She didn't know how to begin.

'You promised me you'd never come back.'

'How could I not?' She knotted her fingers together in front of her to stop herself from reaching out to him. 'I was worried about you.'

He studied her intently for a long moment. And she studied him—he seemed edgier, but as strong as ever. More strong, if that were possible.

'It is okay to break a promise because you care about someone?' he suddenly asked softly. 'Or to lie because you're worried about someone?'

'Some promises aren't right to keep,' she answered with a small shrug. 'And sometimes, yes, you think you're doing the right thing by lying. But generally I think it's better to be honest. Even if it hurts.'

She'd hurt herself, and him, by not being as honest as she should have been right from the start. But she just hadn't been able to be.

'I know you didn't leak my amnesia to the press,' he said decisively. 'I know that, because I did.'

'You leaked your own secret?' She gaped at him. '*Why?* Aren't you worried about how your clients will react?'

He didn't answer her directly. He turned and walked back to his car and picked up a manila file from the front passenger seat. He walked back to the foot of the steps and held it out to her.

'What is it?' she asked as she opened the cover. But it was obvious the second she looked down. It was the paperwork she'd signed less than a week ago.

'The annulment has come through?' she asked dully, not able to force a smile even though it would be the best form of defence. It hurt too much that it was all over between them.

'No.' He picked the pages up, leaving her with an empty folder. 'These haven't been sent in yet.'

'I thought Jasper took them—'

'I got him to bring them back.'

She stared at him, not getting where he was going with this.

'You were right, I have been lying,' he said. 'To myself. And I lied to you too.'

He tore the forms in half. Then he tore them in half again. Then he tossed them to the ground.

'What are you doing?' she shrieked.

'Why didn't you tell me we'd kissed before?'

She didn't answer; she was too busy staring at the shredded pages between their feet.

'When I asked you to tell me about the day we met, you left that out.'

'It wasn't relevant.' She drew breath and looked back into his eyes. 'It was only a minor thing.'

'Was it just a peck on the cheek?'

She froze.

'Or did I kiss you on the mouth?'

She simply couldn't answer.

'Surely you're not *still* shy?' For a split second he actually smiled—that gorgeous teasing, vital smile. Why was he teasing her about this now, when things were so tortured between them?

'I just don't think it's fair that you're a kiss ahead of me,' he added in a low voice. 'I'm going to spend my life trying to catch up.'

Her jaw dropped and she still couldn't get her head around what he was implying. But suddenly he spoke again, and she scrambled to follow what he was telling her.

'I got up early and drove all the way to Durham this morning to see you.' He shoved his hands into his pockets. 'I would have come last night before that story broke, but I had to pre-record an interview and it took longer than we thought. I didn't think you'd see it so quickly. I'm sorry because I wanted to get to you before you read it.'

'Why?' she asked, but the word didn't actually sound.

'When I got to your bedsit at lunchtime, you weren't home and your car wasn't there. I called Jasper and he thought you might be on your way to see me.' He sighed. 'So then I got back in my car and drove all the way home again. I guess I've been slowly catching up to you all day.'

She cleared her throat. 'Why were you coming to see me?'

Did she really have to ask? Tomas looked at her pallor, her wide eyes that revealed so much, and his heart ached.

He didn't want me that way.

He'd never forget the sadness that had sounded in her voice when she'd told him about her husband.

About *himself.*

While he understood the reasons, he hated that she was so insecure and he was so sorry he'd made her feel it all the more. He'd been cruel to her and he knew he didn't deserve her forgiveness. But he was damn well going to fight for it anyway.

'I've worked out what I hate the most about my amnesia.'

She licked her lips. He was mucking this up but he didn't know how else to say it all.

'I can't remember our first kiss,' he muttered, feeling hollow inside. 'That hurts me so much. I don't want to miss any more moments.'

'But—'

'I'm sorry I can't remember the first time we met. How can I not remember our first meeting?' The bereft feeling almost overwhelmed him. 'That's been stolen from me.'

She shook her head. 'I'm *glad* you can't remember.' Her eyes filled. 'You didn't want me then. You wouldn't have loved me then.'

'I kissed you, didn't I?' And that had only been the start.

'Only to say goodbye. Only because you were gallant.'

He almost smiled. 'I was never gallant in all my life. I might not remember much of that time, but I know that for certain. I might not have recognised it then, but there was some fundamental pull between us. I hardly knew you and yet I took one look and married you. That's not the kind of thing I'd do.' He shook his head. 'There was something, there was always something. There had to have been.' He caught her hand as she held it up to stop him. 'I know I can't make you believe me about that back then. But believe me now.'

'Tomas.' The tears trickled down her face. 'You didn't like what you saw in my uncle. In my situation. You saw a way to help me, so you took it. That was all it was. You would have done that for anyone.'

'No, I wouldn't. And even if that were true, then I finally have reason to be glad about the accident. Without this memory loss you might never have come back into my life.' He shook his head. 'That would have been the real tragedy.'

'No.'

He couldn't bear to see the tears spilling from her eyes. She was distraught and it was destroying him inside and he was so screwing this up. 'But I think if I hadn't had the accident I'd have tracked you down anyway. Why else did I get Jasper to delay filing for the annulment if I didn't have some other plan in mind?'

But she shook her head again.

Frustration welled up in him. He needed to make her understand how he felt—what she meant to him. But he'd never opened up to another soul in this way. Never felt this way.

A ring wasn't personal enough for them. Marriage wasn't personal enough—not for them. He wanted to leave an indelible mark on her—brand her as being his. Only his and always his. Because she'd burned her mark on his heart. He might as well tear it from his chest and give it to her on his knees because he was so totally, utterly hers.

Yet at the same time, he never wanted to hurt her or see her hurt again. She was too precious and he didn't know how to keep her close and safe.

He wanted to make her smile again, to make that dimple peep at him and that softly wicked look enter her eyes. But if he had any chance of making that happen, then he had to do the hardest thing and be completely honest with her.

'Tomas?' she murmured as he reached out and framed her face with his hands so he could see into her beautiful eyes and draw the courage he needed from the luminous emotion he saw shining there.

For a second he couldn't speak. He'd been alone all his life. Never more so than in this last year. And oddly, never more so than in this minute. He had only this chance to bridge the gap between them; he needed to do it right.

'I need to tell you the truth,' he confessed, holding her closer. 'I need you to listen. Can you do that?'

'Of course.'

And he needed her to believe him. 'I was horrible and I lied. It's not that I don't trust you. It's that I don't trust myself.'

He dug into his pocket and pulled out a black leather-bound book.

'Read it.' He handed it to her.

'It's your personal journal.'

'Read it.'

Zara nervously opened the journal, reading the entry on the page it had opened to. Dated from a few months ago, it simply detailed all the research he'd done that day. The decisions he'd made. Same with the next entry, and the next, and the next. What soon shone from the pages was the stark lack of interaction with other people. There were emails, occasional phone calls but rarely any meet-ings. Those there were were only with Jasper. She knew he barely met with his household staff. So it wasn't so much what he'd written, but everything that was *missing*. It was just as she'd feared.

'Incredibly boring, isn't it?' He reached across and turned the pages faster. 'Skip a few, they're all the same.'

But she didn't want to read the entries from the last week. From when she was there.

But when she turned to the pages there was only one word written under each date.

Zara.

'I couldn't capture it then,' he explained in a low voice. 'I couldn't face it myself, let alone write it. Turn to today.'

Apologise. Bring her back. Love her.

He closed the book and dropped it to the ground, step-ping closer to her at the same time. 'I sent you away be-cause I was trying to do the right thing but I did it horribly. I made you think I didn't care. I deliberately said things I knew would hurt you most because I wanted to drive you away. I wanted to hurt you so you'd hate me. So you'd turn and leave and never come back. But now here you are, back again.' He smiled sadly. 'Because you were con-cerned about me?'

She nodded.

'Because you love me?'

'Yes,' she whispered. 'But you don't believe me.'

'I don't deserve your love, Zara. But I'm going to take it. And I'm never giving it up again.' He held her so she couldn't step away. 'I'm never letting you go again.'

She pressed her hand to her mouth, trying to hold back

her sobs, because it was so important she listen and hear him. She ached to understand.

'I'm terrified of losing more. Of losing all *this*. The mornings are the worst. I wake up and then remember how much I've lost. Every day it's like a weight that gets dumped on me, dragging me down. But that morning I woke up with you beside me and it was the best morning that I can remember ever. It didn't matter any more because you were there smiling at me.'

She remembered his smile. The way he'd held her. She remembered the sheer joyous vitality pouring from his body.

'But then Jasper arrived,' she said.

'I felt betrayed.' He nodded. 'I hated that you knew all this stuff I'd missed. It crystallised all my worst fears. But most of all I was so bitterly disappointed. There was a part of me who'd wanted what I shared with you to be new and fresh. I hoped that you could accept me as I am now, that you'd never really know how broken I was. But you knew exactly how broken I was. You knew me from before. And I didn't want you lumbered with someone so...' He trailed off.

Her heart broke for him.

'You'd had enough of a rough time trapped in a horrible environment. You don't need a man who isn't one hundred per cent. Someone who...'

'Tomas—'

'But I'm selfish. I'm so selfish. And I want you too much. I don't want to let you go even when I know I should. I used to hope it would come back. I need to lose that hope. Just as I need to lose the fear I might lose more of my memory. I need to stop hiding and live now,' he said. 'You showed me everything I'm missing out on and now I want it all. I want you with me. I was afraid of waking up and not remembering you. But waking up now and not having you with me is a nightmare. I'm living one without you. I can't bear to wake up tomorrow morning and not have you be the first thing I see. Nothing is right when I don't see you first thing. I need you next to me.'

'Tomas—'

'I love you, Zara. I'm sorry I drove you away. I've never regretted anything more. It is the worst thing in the world when a person you love leaves you. I know this too well and I'm sorry I hurt you.'

But she needed to tell him the truth too. 'It's so awful of me but there's a part of me that's glad you can't remember that day. I don't want you to know how truly weak I was then. I *hate* how I was then.' She hated that she hadn't had the strength to leave of her own accord. That she'd needed his help.

'You would have rescued yourself eventually,' he said.

Would she? These things took a strength that was hard to come by. Hard when you'd been through years of being belittled. Undervalued. Unloved.

And people wanted love. People put up with all kinds of horrible for the paltry bit of love thrown their way. People clung on in the hope that it would get better. She'd been that person. She'd tried so hard for so long because she'd wanted that approval and that love.

She'd wanted what she'd lost when her parents had died. That security and safety and sense of belonging.

'You're more resourceful than you like to believe. Stronger than you know. But back then you were alone and unloved and a bit damaged.' He lifted a shoulder. 'But, you know, I'm a bit damaged too. That's okay. We're still okay.'

She looked into his eyes. He was so very right.

'Can you just hold me?' she begged.

His arms came around her and she cried. He held her close, rocking her gently as she let go of all the awful tension and doubt.

'I'm so sorry.' She sniffed. 'I've made your shirt all wet.'

'Never apologise,' he whispered. 'Stay with me now.'

She could finally smile. Finally believe it. 'Will you come back into the world more with me?'

'Haven't I already? The whole world knows the truth about me now.'

'You did that because of me?'

He nodded. 'I want to stop hiding. Stop being afraid. And I know you need more of the world because you were constrained for so long by your uncle. So we don't have to stay here at Raxworthy if you don't want to.'

Her jaw dropped. 'I adore this home and I'd love nothing more than to live here with you.' Frankly she'd live anywhere with him.

'You'll work on your business?'

'Just try and stop me.'

He grinned, the tension finally easing in his features. 'Thank goodness. I love being your guinea pig.'

She cupped his jaw with her hand. 'Maybe we could throw open the gates and show the gardens again. Just once a month.' They could let the world in, just a little.

'But how are we to bathe naked in the glasshouse if there might be people about to see?'

She laughed. 'One afternoon's abstinence will be a sacrifice, I admit.'

'We'll have to go somewhere for that weekend—Venice, New York, Paris...'

She couldn't stop the huge smile from spreading across her features. 'That sounds like a *really* good idea.'

'I've got another one.' He leaned closer.

'Full of them this afternoon, aren't you?'

'Uh-huh.' He nodded, but his expression turned serious. 'The gardens will be beautiful in spring.' He gazed at her. 'I think you would look lovely walking towards me in that garden.' He inclined his head. 'Maybe you'd wear a dress.'

'I get to be in clothes now?' she teased. 'Why would I be walking towards you in a dress?'

'For our marriage blessing,' he answered softly. 'And we'll reaffirm our vows so I can remember them this time.' He brushed his finger across her lips. 'I'll mean them differently this time. And I'll mean them for ever.'

She smiled at him. 'I'll say them every day to you if you need me to.'

'Yes.' He dropped to his knees. 'So will you marry me, Zara? Even though we're already married?' He smiled ruefully.

She loved that he could laugh about it with her. But more than that he was giving her that moment that she'd not had last time.

'Yes.' She bent and took his face in her hands and kissed him tenderly. 'And you'll make the most of the moments with me?'

'Zara. I love you,' he said simply as he stood. 'And I will love you every moment of every day for the rest of my life.'

She wrapped her arms around him tightly, unable to speak for the joy flowing through her. They'd both been alone but they had this second chance. They had each other. And then the magic was back—those long, luscious kisses that she couldn't get enough of. She leaned back against the door for support as he soothed her soul—then stirred it to new heights as their passion exploded.

'What are you doing?' she gasped as he unexpectedly broke the kiss and lifted her into his arms.

'I'm carrying my bride over the threshold,' he answered, tossing her a little higher, then tighter in his arms. 'It's a bit belated, but I'm taking the moment.'

'What other moments do you have in mind?'

'I'm going to close the door and press my wife up against it and have my way with her here and now because I cannot wait a second longer.'

'That sounds like a good moment.' She smiled at him.
'It'll be the first of millions,' he promised.
'Yes,' she vowed. 'Yes, yes, yes.'

* * * * *

*If you enjoyed this story, why not explore
Natalie Anderson's fabulous duet*
THE THRONE OF SAN FELIPE?

*THE SECRET THAT SHOCKED DE SANTIS
THE MISTRESS THAT TAMED DE SANTIS*

Available now!

MILLS & BOON®
Hardback – March 2017

ROMANCE

Secrets of a Billionaire's Mistress	Sharon Kendrick
Claimed for the De Carrillo Twins	Abby Green
The Innocent's Secret Baby	Carol Marinelli
The Temporary Mrs Marchetti	Melanie Milburne
A Debt Paid in the Marriage Bed	Jennifer Hayward
The Sicilian's Defiant Virgin	Susan Stephens
Pursued by the Desert Prince	Dani Collins
The Forgotten Gallo Bride	Natalie Anderson
Return of Her Italian Duke	Rebecca Winters
The Millionaire's Royal Rescue	Jennifer Faye
Proposal for the Wedding Planner	Sophie Pembroke
A Bride for the Brooding Boss	Bella Bucannon
Their Secret Royal Baby	Carol Marinelli
Her Hot Highland Doc	Annie O'Neil
His Pregnant Royal Bride	Amy Ruttan
Baby Surprise for the Doctor Prince	Robin Gianna
Resisting Her Army Doc Rival	Susan MacKay
A Month to Marry the Midwife	Fiona McArthur
Billionaire's Baby Promise	Sarah M. Anderson
Seduce Me, Cowboy	Maisey Yates

MILLS & BOON®
Large Print – March 2017

ROMANCE

Di Sione's Virgin Mistress	Sharon Kendrick
Snowbound with His Innocent Temptation	Cathy Williams
The Italian's Christmas Child	Lynne Graham
A Diamond for Del Rio's Housekeeper	Susan Stephens
Claiming His Christmas Consequence	Michelle Smart
One Night with Gael	Maya Blake
Married for the Italian's Heir	Rachael Thomas
Christmas Baby for the Princess	Barbara Wallace
Greek Tycoon's Mistletoe Proposal	Kandy Shepherd
The Billionaire's Prize	Rebecca Winters
The Earl's Snow-Kissed Proposal	Nina Milne

HISTORICAL

The Runaway Governess	Liz Tyner
The Winterley Scandal	Elizabeth Beacon
The Queen's Christmas Summons	Amanda McCabe
The Discerning Gentleman's Guide	Virginia Heath

MEDICAL

A Daddy for Her Daughter	Tina Beckett
Reunited with His Runaway Bride	Robin Gianna
Rescued by Dr Rafe	Annie Claydon
Saved by the Single Dad	Annie Claydon
Sizzling Nights with Dr Off-Limits	Janice Lynn
Seven Nights with Her Ex	Louisa Heaton